THE PERSON CONTROLLER

PRESS A+B+UP+DOWN TO UNLOCK HILARIOUS BOOK MODE

DAVID BADDIEL is an author and comedian. His debut children's novel *The Parent Agency* was the bestselling 9-12 debut of 2014 and was hailed by the *Guardian* as "funny, sometimes moving and always engaging."

The Person Controller is his second novel – and it confirms David as a brilliant and original new voice in children's fiction.

Books by David Baddiel

THE PARENT AGENCY
THE PERSON CONTROLLER
ANIMALCOLM
BIRTHDAY BOY

THE PERSON CONTROLLER

PRESS A+B+UP+DOWN TO UNLOCK HILARIOUS BOOK MODE

DAVID BADDIEL

Illustrated by Jim Field

HarperCollins *Children's Books*

First published in hardback in Great Britain by HarperCollins *Children's Books* 2015
First published in paperback in Great Britain by HarperCollins *Children's Books* 2016
HarperCollins *Children's Books* is a division of HarperCollins*Publishers* Ltd
1 London Bridge Street, London SE1 9GF

Visit us on the web at
www.harpercollins.co.uk

HarperCollinsPublishers
1st Floor, Watemarque Building, Ringsend Road
Dublin 4, Ireland

25

Text copyright © David Baddiel 2015
Illustrations copyright © Jim Field 2015

David Baddiel and Jim Field assert the moral right
to be identified as the author and illustrator of the work

ISBN: 978-0-00-755454-6

Printed and bound by
CPI Group (UK) Ltd, Croydon, CR0 4YY

To the Grandmas — Sarah, and Dinks,
late of this parish.

PART 1

PAUSE

CHAPTER 1
Fred and Ellie

Fred and Ellie Stone were twins. But they were never sure whether or not they could call themselves identical. They certainly shared exactly the same birthday (20th September, eleven years ago) and they had the same mum and dad (Eric and Janine). But their names were Fred and Ellie. And a boy and a girl are, clearly, not identical.[1]

Yet they *felt* identical. They sometimes even felt

---

[1] A boy and girl can only be fraternal twins, never identical. But don't ask me to explain the difference. It's a bit yucky.

that they knew what one another were thinking. And, even if they were 200 metres apart, they could mouth words at each other and always know what the other one was saying. They did look pretty identical too. They

both wore glasses and, most of the time, their school uniforms (even though uniform wasn't compulsory at their school). And they both, at the point at which this story begins, had braces on their top teeth.

They also both *liked* the same things. These included: superheroes; Japanese fantasy animation films; comics; maths (yes, they actually *liked* maths –

sometimes they played a game called 'Who Can Name More Decimal Places of Pi?'); and, most importantly, video games. *All* video games, but their favourites were *FIFA*, *Street Fighter*, *Super Mario* and *Minecraft*. The one thing they would save up their not-very-much pocket money to buy was the most up-to-date versions of these games. Ellie, though, was better than Fred at video games.[2] Which Fred didn't mind. He knew she had quicker fingers and better hand-to-eye coordination.

---

[2] Fred was better than her at one thing, however: customising the avatars. He could customise any avatar on any game so the character on screen looked great – hairstyle, eye colour, skin colour, clothes, teeth, every shape and size. Fred sometimes wondered if he didn't like doing that even more than playing the games.

And, even though he sometimes got frustrated at losing, other times he just liked watching her fingers speed across her controller, as if she was playing a classical concerto by heart. And, when I say her controller, I mean *her* controller. Ellie and Fred always used their own ones. Ellie in particular was always very definite about which one was hers. The feel and the weight of her controller – even if, to the untrained eye/hand, both of them may have looked/felt exactly the same – suited her style perfectly.

Which was why what happened to it was quite so upsetting.

CHAPTER 2
Eric

Eric Stone was – there is no nice way of saying this – fat. Well, there *are* nice ways of saying it – and Eric did often use these ways, describing himself as *big-boned*, or *portly*, or suffering from *terrible water retention* – but the truth was he was fat. Because he ate too much. He didn't have terrible water retention; he had terrible bacon-sandwich retention.

To be fair to Eric, he did – normally after a bit of prompting from his wife, Janine, and his children,

15

Fred and Ellie – go on a lot of diets.

He'd been on the High Fibre diet, and the Low Carb diet, and the Juice diet, and the No Juice diet, and the Cabbage Soup diet, and the Pea and Mint Soup diet, and a diet he made up where he only ate banana muffins and cheese. He'd been on the 5:2 diet and the 6:1 diet and the 4:3 diet and the 2:5 diet and even the 17:28 diet (which meant not

eating anything for a minute between 17:27 and 17:29 every day). He'd been to Weight Watchers and Chocaholics Anonymous and Sixteen-stoners' Self-help and Big-boned Portly Bacon Sandwich Retentors Sit Around in a Circle and Say How it isn't Really Their Fault (actually this last one was what Janine called *all* Eric's diet groups).

Trouble was, the diets didn't make Eric any lighter. If anything, they made him heavier because every time he finished one – and he did *always* finish them, normally after only four or five days – he would eat about five times his own weight in bacon sandwiches.[3]

Eric was just tucking into a bacon sandwich – the first one he'd had after giving up on the Jacket Potato Skin diet, which he'd followed for two whole

---

[3] It didn't help that Eric worked for a supermarket as a retail manager, whatever that is (I should know, I know, but I don't – I've never known what jobs called things like that actually involve). This meant the Stones got large discounts on all their food, especially bacon, and Eric brought home so much of it that he got a discount on his discount.

days (it allowed you to eat jacket potato skins and you could put low-fat spread on them, which Eric had decided included mayonnaise) – when *it*, the thing that happened to Ellie's controller which was so upsetting, happened.[4]

The bacon sandwich, in a way, was what caused the whole thing. Because, whenever Eric Stone had his first bacon sandwich after a diet, he would become so entranced by the fatty saltiness of the pork rashers and how deliciously it sat against the brown-sauce-smeared white bread that he would forget everything else and close his eyes. He would lose himself in that bacon sandwich.

Unfortunately, the point at which he was losing himself in this *particular* bacon sandwich was also the point at which he was sitting down, on the sofa, in front of the TV, plate in one hand, sandwich in the other, IN HIS PANTS.

His big, grey, bought-in-1987 Y-front PANTS.

---

[4] I'm aware that there are two uses of the word 'happened' very close together here. Don't let it worry you.

He had been planning to open his eyes shortly and watch TV. But not for a little while. Not until he'd really savoured the saltiness. Not until...

"Ow!!!" said Eric, opening his eyes very wide.

"What is it?" said Janine, not bothering to turn away from *Cash in the Attic*. Janine Stone never missed an episode and was convinced that one day she herself would find something in the attic worth millions of pounds. Which was odd, as the Stone family lived in a ground-floor flat.

"I've sat on something, J!" said Eric.

"Well, move off it then," said Janine, still looking at the screen while stroking the family cat, a white fluffy beast called Margaret Scratcher.

"I can't!"

"You can't?"

"I think... I think it's stuck!"

Eric stood up.

He turned round, facing away from his wife. Interestingly, despite the obvious pain he was in, at no point did he stop eating his bacon sandwich.

"Can you see it?" he said.

"What do you mean can I see it?"

He glanced over his shoulder. "Stop watching *Cash in the Attic*! Just for a second!"

With a big *tut*, Janine Stone forced her eyes away from the television and looked across Margaret Scratcher's fur at her husband's back. Then she lowered her gaze a fraction.

"What's that?" she said.

"What's what?"

"That black thing. Poking out of your pants."

"That's what I want to know!" said Eric. "Never mind it poking out, it's poking *me*!"

There was another *tut* from behind him. Eric had once admitted – quietly, to his friends in his works canteen, over a bacon sandwich – that if his wife was a noise, she would be a *tut*.

"For pity's sake, Eric. Bend over."

Eric did as he was told. There was a short pause as Janine – and Margaret Scratcher – peered. Eric felt he could *hear* them peering. Then she said: "How on earth did you get *that* stuck up there?"

"How on earth did I get *what* stuck up there?"

"MY VIDEO-GAME CONTROLLER!!!" said another voice.

Ellie's voice in fact. Sounding very upset. Reasonably, really, since she had just come into the living room to see her mother reaching out a slightly disgusted hand to retrieve her most prized possession from between the cheeks of her father's 1987 Y-front-panted bottom.

CHAPTER 3
Cyberdodo

As it happened, Ellie's controller wasn't actually broken. The toggle had gone a touch floppy and the X button looked like it had been knocked diagonal by whatever G-force it sustained while between Eric's bottom cheeks. But it worked, kind of. If you ignored the fact that when it shuddered – like controllers do when you hit the bar in *FIFA*, or there's an explosion in *Call of Duty* – it felt, to Ellie, like it was shuddering for another reason.

That reason being that it had been lost, for a short while, in a very bad place.

Basically, Ellie just didn't really want to touch her beloved controller any more. Which everyone in the family, including Eric, understood. In fact, Eric, who was a nice person and a good dad – even if he loved bacon sandwiches almost as much as his children – went so far as to tell Ellie that he was perfectly willing to pay for a new controller. As long as she didn't tell anyone what had happened to the old one.

The day after Eric made that promise, Fred and Ellie were in their school computer room. Well, it wasn't really a computer *room*. Bracket Wood was a good school – more or less – but it didn't have any money. And so what it called a computer room was in fact a cleaning cupboard with all the cleaning materials taken out and an eight-year-old laptop on the shelf where there used to be five half-full bottles of Toilet Duck.

However, Fred and Ellie didn't mind. Because right then they were enjoying going through all their favourite gaming sites and reading reviews of all the latest controllers. Ellie, in particular, was *really* enjoying herself.

"People who aren't gamers don't know this, do they?" she was saying. "They think that controllers just come in black plastic with some buttons, bundled with a console. But they're so wrong! Look!"

Fred, who tended just to listen when Ellie got very excited about anything to do with gaming, nodded. She was right. Clicking quickly through many different web pages – her skill at video games showing in how expert she also was with a mouse – she pulled up on the screen *loads* of different types of controller.

Black ones, grey ones, silver ones, rainbow ones,

camouflage ones, football team colours ones; ones with big toggles, small toggles, toggles that were gear sticks and steering wheels; controllers with blue lights and white lights and red lights and yellow lights; with ribbed handles and smooth handles and leather-clad handles and handles shaped like hands; with headphones and microphones and speakers attached; and ones you could personalise yourself – you could even have one made in the shape of your own name!

"The two Ls in Ellie could be the handles!" she said excitedly.

"Yes!" said Fred, wondering how that would work with 'Fred'. Maybe if he went for Frederick the k and the d could be the handles... but, then again, *Frederick* was probably a bit long for a video-game controller. He'd have to hold his hands really wide apart.

"What browser are you using?" said their sort-of friend Stirling, one of the few other pupils at Bracket

Wood who could often be found in the computer room. He was standing behind Ellie, peering at the screen.

"Browser?" said Ellie, not turning round. "I dunno. Safari?"

Stirling looked at his younger sister, Scarlet. They burst out laughing.

"*Safari!* Oh dear! Oh dear! Oh dear!" they said together.

Ellie raised her eyes at Fred, who raised his own back. Stirling and Scarlet were *very* technologically aware and *very* proud of it. This was one reason why, as far as Fred and Ellie were concerned, they were sort-of friends, rather than friends.[5]

"Is that wrong?" said Ellie.

"Well, it's not wrong, but if you want to be truly up to speed…" said Stirling.

---

[5] Another reason was their challenging hair. Stirling and Scarlet's mum had recently married a new husband, who was a hairdresser. His name was Mr Bodzharov and his proud motto was: "I cut hair" [including his stepchildren's] "like they used to in the Old Country!" I'll leave you to imagine what this means.

"...both design-wise and speed-wise," said Scarlet. "As in download speed," she added helpfully.

"Then I think we would suggest, wouldn't we, Scarlet...?"

Scarlet nodded eagerly. "...Allegro?" she said. "Quicksmart? Protickle? Internet Wing-Ding? Paloma's World? Browzzzer?"

"All great," said Stirling. "But for me, top of the browser tree has to be, at this moment in time, Cyberdodo!"

"Oh, of course, Cyberdodo!"

"Never heard of it," said Ellie.

"Where does it say that? Twitter?" said Fred.

"Twitter? Oh dear! Oh dear! Oh dear!" they went.

"What are you, a *pensioner*?" added Stirling. "No, Cyberdodo is what everyone recommends on..."

"...Instantgone?" said Scarlet. "Wizzstream? Quack? FaceTunnel? Pinterestingenough? Derkanpooderleck?"

Stirling shook his head. "...ChatWhiskers!"

"ChatWhiskers! Of course!"

Ellie, who had continued to stare at the screen while all this was going on, turned round at last. "Stirling. Scarlet. Can I ask you a question? Are you even *on* social media?"

They looked at each other. Then shook their heads.

"Are you in fact even allowed to *use* a computer without your parents' supervision?"

Scarlet and Stirling looked at each other again. Then shook their heads.

"Our mum says we can when we're in Year Five," said Scarlet quietly.

This was the other reason that Stirling and Scarlet were only *sort-of* friends: they were in Years Three and Two. They were eight and seven.

"OK, iBabies…" said Ellie, turning back round to the computer. "Then perhaps some of your recommendations can wait. At least until…"

"Well, well, well."

This wasn't said by Stirling or Scarlet. In fact, when Ellie and Fred turned round, Stirling and Scarlet had vanished.

Standing there instead were the other twins in the school: Isla and Morris Fawcett.

"Oh no," said Fred.

CHAPTER 4
The other twins

Like Fred and Ellie, Isla and Morris were twins; but also like them, a boy and a girl and therefore, also, non-identical twins. But, unlike Fred and Ellie, they were really *obviously* non-identical. Isla was very, very pretty, tall for her age and slim, with blue eyes and a tiny nose and long hair that she would sometimes sweep back across her face as if she was in a shampoo advert.

Morris looked like a badly shaven gorilla.

New pupils at the school, therefore, tended to be frightened of Morris. Which they were right to be. But the person they *really* needed to be frightened of was Isla.

Because Morris and Isla Fawcett were the Bracket Wood school bullies. They prided themselves on it. They spent a lot of time working on their bullying style. They had even been heard to talk about their bullying *brand*. And within that brand, although Morris did more of the actual physical work – he covered Chinese burns, dead legs and wedgies – it was Isla who was the mastermind.[6]

"Go away," said Ellie.

"I don't think so," said Isla, reaching over and turning the laptop screen towards her and her brother.

"OoooOOOOooooo!!" they said, both going up sarcastically on the middle OOOO.

Ellie raised her eyes to heaven. "How long have you two been practising that?" she said.

"About three day—"

"Shut up, Morris!" said Isla. "Anyway, I see you're looking for video-game stuff, are you?"

"Yeah! Are you?" said Morris, who tended, when not exactly sure what to do re the whole bullying thing, just to repeat what Isla said.

---

[6] It has to be said that they were pretty successful bullies. At most schools these days, bullies are very quickly clamped down on by the teachers. But at Bracket Wood, although it was a good school – more or less – no one had really clamped down on Morris and Isla Fawcett. Perhaps you might understand why this was when I tell you that the headmaster's name was Stephen Fawcett.

"Well spotted!" said Ellie. "Thank God there's a photo on the screen so that you could work that out. How would you have known if it was just words?"

"Very funny..." said Isla. "At least I can see it without glasses."

"There's nothing wrong with wearing glasses!"

"Oh, isn't there? Shall we go and ask Rashid? If he likes *girls with glasses*? Or, for that matter, girls with *braces* and *pigtails* and *who still dress like they're in Year One*...?"

Ellie blushed and looked away.

Rashid Khan was universally considered to be the most handsome boy in their class. More importantly, he was also universally considered to be the nicest boy in their class.

Now, Ellie wasn't very interested in boys – she was much more interested in video games – but something about Rashid did make her feel a bit funny inside. A long time ago – back in Year Four, before Isla Fawcett had completely grown into the bully she now was – Ellie had stupidly confided this to her and now she was always worried that one day Isla was going to tell Rashid. Who, Ellie was sure, probably liked Isla, or at least girls who looked like Isla, more than Ellie anyway.

Fred, knowing that the mention of Rashid had embarrassed his sister, said: "Leave it, Isla."

"Sorry, what was that?" said Isla, turning to him.

"Yeah, what was that?" said Morris, also turning to him.

It was true Fred hadn't said it very loudly.

"Nothing," said Fred.

"Oh, that's very odd," said Isla.

"Yeah. Odd. Very," said Morris, improvising.

"Because I'm sure you said something. Was it maybe… something about being a *boy* who isn't even as good at video games as his *sister*…?"

"Yeah! His *sister*!" said Morris.

Fred looked away, embarrassed.

Even though he didn't mind at all that his sister was better than him at video games, he did mind people at school making fun of him for it. Which some did. Not because Ellie had told everyone, but because Eric, at Bracket Wood's last parent-teacher evening, when asked by their form teacher, Miss Parr, what he thought Ellie's particular talents were, had said: "Video games. You'd have thought that would've been the boy, but no, she's the one with the magic fingers!!"

Unfortunately, Eric's voice was very loud and booming, and everyone in their form room – and most of the rest of the school – had heard.

"In fact, Fred, you're probably even worse at video games than you are at actual games!" said Isla.

"Yeah! Actual games!" said Morris.

"Like…" said Isla, turning to Morris.

There was a pause.

"What?" said Morris.

"I thought *you* might say this bit," said Isla.

Morris frowned. "What bit?"

"The bit about which games he's rubbish at...? Like, give some examples?"

Morris looked blank.

"Oh, come on, Morris!" said Isla. "Do you have any idea how hard it is to always *drive* the bullying? To have to come up with all the clever things to say to humiliate other children? Frankly, I'm starting to think you're just a passenger in what we're doing here."

Morris frowned again. Then he frowned some more. Finally, his face cleared. "Football!" he said, clicking his fingers.

"Yes! Well *done*, Morris! Yeah! What are you worse at, Fred – *FIFA* or football? You could hardly be worse at *FIFA* – because I've never seen *anyone* so bad at football!"

"Yeah, so bad at football!" said Morris.

"Oh, shut up!" said Ellie, getting up to face the bullies.

"Yeah, shut up!" said Fred, getting up and facing them too. He had had enough.

Because football meant a lot to Fred. He wanted more than anything to be in the Bracket Wood First XI. He wanted to be in the Bracket Wood First XI and score the winning goal in the final of the Bracket Wood and Surrounding Area Inter-school Winter Trophy. Ever since he was old enough, he had gone to the school trials for the team. And every year he hadn't got in. Every year something had gone wrong.

Let's just take a moment out from the main story to look at the last time Fred went to one of the trials for the school football team.

CHAPTER 5
Fred's football trials: just one example

This was last year, when Fred was in Year Five. For the trial, Fred had spent all his pocket money on a new pair of football boots. Bright yellow ones. *Marauders*. Fred was totally convinced that they were going to make all the difference (to the fact that he hadn't been picked on any of the three preceding years).

Unfortunately, Eric and Janine had never taught Fred how to tie his shoelaces properly.[7] So what normally happened was that every morning, before school, Ellie would tie Fred's school shoes very, very tightly with a triple bow. And that would be fine; they would stay tied for the whole day.

But, before the school team trial, Fred had asked Ellie to tie his Marauders with just a single bow. Because a triple bow, he thought, would be too bulky and make it very difficult – for example – when the ball came to him on the edge of the penalty area to bend it round five defenders into the top right-hand corner (not something he had ever done, but he was sure he was going to this time).

"Really?" said Ellie, kneeling down by the touchline of the school pitch. I say school pitch. And touchline. Bracket Wood was a good school

---

[7] They had, to be fair, at the time when both their children needed to be thinking about tying their own shoelaces, bought a big, flat, cardboard training shoe. Like this one:

This had worked for Ellie. But Fred was never able to transfer big, flat training shoelace-tying to real, 3D shoelace-tying.

– more or less – but its school pitch was a muddy triangle in the local park and its touchline was the concrete path around it.

"Really," said Fred. "A single knot." And ran on. And, as his laces came untied, tripped over. Into some mud.

And then ran backwards and forwards to the touchline throughout the game so that Ellie could retie his shoelaces.

He did stop doing that eventually. Because, after the fifth time, Ellie said: "If you're not going to let me tie a triple knot, I'm not tying them at all any more!!" and went to sit on the roundabout in the playground six metres away.

After which Fred had to ask the referee, Mr Barrington, to tie his shoelaces. Bracket Wood was a good school – more or less – but its sports teacher was Mr Barrington, who was sixty-seven and wore glasses with lenses thicker than a rhinoceros's foot.

So after Mr Barrington had sighed very heavily

and bent down on one knee in the mud to tie up Fred's shoelaces – and after it had taken him three minutes to get up again, during which time four goals were scored that never got recorded – he made a point of running (well, staggering) away every time Fred approached him.

Fred didn't know what to do. His boots kept on coming off. Briefly, he even wished his mum or dad was there, which was something he didn't often wish for.

Then, eventually, Ellie came back from the playground and Fred let her tie the Marauder shoelaces into a triple bow. Two minutes later, the ball came to him on the edge of the penalty area.

"Come on, Fred!" shouted Ellie. "Hit it!"

Fred focused on the ball. He ran towards it, confident now that his shoelaces were not going to come undone. He hit the ball square in the middle of his left boot.

Square in the middle of his triple bow.

So the ball went almost nowhere near his actual foot. It went almost entirely near the big knot of his shoelace. Fred, to be fair, had been right. A bow that size *was* too bulky. Which wasn't much comfort to him as the ball spun backwards over his head, hitting Mr Barrington full in the face.

"Ow!!!" said Mr Barrington, as his rhino-foot-lens glasses flew off his face and into the mud.

Everyone apart from Fred laughed, loud and long. Fred himself just turned and walked off, knowing that he certainly wasn't going to get into the school team this time.

Now let's go back to the main story.

CHAPTER 6
Wedgie

So *that's* why Isla and Morris making fun of his footballing ability did touch a nerve with Fred. And why he told them to shut up.

It felt good, saying shut up. It felt, to Fred, that the time had come to stand up and be counted, and he had stood up and been counted. He had said: *This much and no more.* He had drawn a line in the sand and told the bullies not to cross it.

And that feeling – that he had stood up and been

counted, that he had said this much and no more, that he had drawn a line in the sand and told the bullies not to cross it – was certainly some small comfort to Fred as Morris proceeded to give him a dead leg, an elbow drill and a wedgie.

CHAPTER 7
CLICK HERE

"I feel really bad," said Ellie, trying to help Fred out of the dustbin. (Isla and Morris's last move, a classic bit of bullying, was to plonk Fred in the computer-room bin bottom first, so that his legs stuck out like wheelbarrow handles.)

"Don't feel really bad," said Fred.

"What did you say?" said Ellie.

"I said…" said Fred, trying hard this time not to groan as he said it, "don't feel really bad."

"But I'm your sister." She grabbed hold of his legs and pulled. "And just because I'm a girl shouldn't mean that I can't protect you from the bullies and…"

As she spoke, her weight finally pulled her brother – and the bin attached to his bum, looking not unlike a snail's shell – forward. Two seconds later, the bin clattered to the floor, popping

Fred out as it went. He picked himself up.

"I know that, Ellie. But you tried your best. It wasn't your fault that Isla's arm is quite long."

This was a reference to the fact that, while Fred was getting his dead leg and his elbow drill and his wedgie, Isla had been holding an arm out and blocking Ellie from getting close enough to help her brother by putting her palm on Ellie's forehead. Ellie had swung her arms a few times, but sadly got nowhere near landing any punches.

"Anyway, where's the laptop?" Fred said.

They both looked around. It wasn't on the shelf any more. It was on the floor next to some scrunched-up sweet wrappers that had fallen out of the bin. It had landed upside down, in the shape of a tiny tent.

"Oh my God!" said Ellie.

She lifted it up carefully, as if it was a bird whose wings had folded down across its body after an injury. But it was fine when she turned it round.

More than fine actually. The screen seemed to be glowing brighter than ever.

And on the screen the browser had clicked through to a new page on which was shown this:

It was an amazing-looking controller. It was black, but with blue lines running across its body. There weren't four buttons on the top right-hand side, as normal, but six; and they weren't lettered, or numbered, or ordinary colours: red and green and yellow. They were *jewelled*: silver and gold and diamond and emerald and amber and ruby.

The control stick, which also had a jewelled top, appeared to be reaching out of the screen, as if in 3D.

Its central button had no recognisable trademark, but just an image of something. It might have been a person, or an animal, or a ghost dancing.

"Wow…" said Fred.

"Yeah. Wow…" said Ellie. She clicked on the screen for a closer view.

At which point the blue lines running across the body of the controller lit up and began to pulse. The blue light washed across Ellie and Fred's spellbound faces.

"What *is* this website?" said Fred.

"I don't know." Ellie was still staring enraptured at the screen. "But I do know that this… is *my* controller."

"Really?" said Fred.

"Yes," said Ellie. "I can feel it."

Fred nodded. He knew there was no point in arguing with Ellie when she had set her mind on something.

"OK… but… how do we pay for it?"

Ellie frowned. "Uh…"

A link popped up that simply said:

CLICK HERE.

So she did.

There was a moment of computer fuzz. And then, in a little window next to the controller, a man, bald but with long hair at the back, wearing very small square sunglasses and a head mic, appeared on screen. He looked directly at the twins.

"I am… oh blast. Wait a minute." He flicked a switch on his head mic.

"I am…" he said again, but now his voice had a slight electronic echo, "…the Mystery Man!!"

Fred and Ellie exchanged glances.

"Right…" said Ellie. "Nice to meet you."

The man nodded. There was a long pause. The

Mystery Man seemed to be sizing them up from inside the screen. Eventually, he said, "Answer me this: are you nerds?"

"Sorry?" said Ellie.

"Are you... NERDS?!!" he said, more loudly.

Fred and Ellie looked at each other. They took in each other's V-necks, glasses and braces. They thought for a moment about their joint liking for superheroes, comics, Japanese fantasy animation films, maths and video games. And they realised that the answer was:

"Well, yes. I suppose so," said Ellie.

"Yes, I suppose so too," said Fred.

"No, that's not good enough," said the Mystery Man from the laptop screen. "You need to say it loud and say it proud. You need to own it. So once more: are you... NERDS?!"

Fred and Ellie looked at each other again. Ellie shrugged.

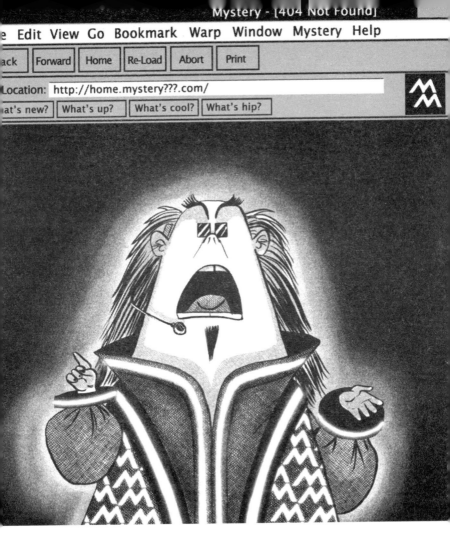

"Actually," she said, "we've got these other friends…"

"*Sort-of* friends," said Fred.

"…yes… and they're probably *more* nerdy than us…"

"The iBabies? They're too young," said the Mystery Man. "I'm not interested in them."

Ellie made a face. "Rude," she said.

"Can we get on?" said the Mystery Man. "Are you or are you not… NERDS?!"

Fred and Ellie looked at each other for a third time. They didn't have to speak to each other to know what they were going to do.

"YES!" they said, turning back to the screen. "WE ARE NERDS!!"

The Mystery Man nodded, seeming finally satisfied. He reached down somewhere below the little window and pressed a button. A mysterious-sounding chord – like something from the soundtrack of an old horror film – played tinnily.

"Then you, Ellie and Fred Stone…" the Mystery Man continued, "…are the new owners of… the Controller!!!"

CHAPTER 8
Say please

The Mystery Man reached down and played the chord again. When it was over, Ellie said: "How do you know our names?"

"Or," said Fred, "Scarlet and Stirling's ages?"

"Or the fact that we call them the iBabies?"

"Do not ask questions of the Mystery Man," he intoned solemnly.

"What's your real name?" said Fred.

"My real name is the Mystery Man. And that is a

question. And I have told you not to ask questions of the Mystery Man…"

"You answered it, though," said Ellie.

"Shut up," said the Mystery Man crossly.

"But how do you know our names?"

The Mystery Man sighed and made a wavy, flicky gesture with his hand, like people do when they want to suggest that the things you're asking just aren't important. "You may as well ask how I, a face on the screen, am able to converse with you, two flesh-and-blood people."

"Well," said Ellie, "I assume it's because you're on some sort of webcam."

The Mystery Man rolled his eyes. "Look. Do you want the Controller or not?"

"Are you saying we've already bought it?"

"You're asking questions again! Goodness!"

"But did we pay for it? How did we pay for it just by clicking on the picture?" said Fred.

"Look. These are all *questions*. I'm not supposed to answer questions. But… consider it a free trial. OK?"

Fred frowned. He could feel without looking at her – because they were twins – that Ellie was smiling. In fact, he could feel without looking at her that Ellie was just going to really happily say, "Yes, OK!"

But he wasn't sure they should be accepting strange gadgets from strange men on the internet. Even if the gadget did look kind of amazing. So he was about to say, "Hold on a minute, Ellie…" when he heard a voice from the corridor outside.

"No, Morris… a bully claps *sarcastically*. And slowly…"

Fred turned. He could hear footsteps from around the corner.

"Ellie," he said. "Isla and Morris are coming back…"

"Oh! What shall we do?" said Ellie.

"Just say, 'Yes, OK!' That's what you were going to say anyway!!!"

"*Sar-cas-tickly*," said Morris, still outside the room but much closer now. "Right. And slowly." Then came the sound of him practising his clapping.

"Just do it!" Fred hissed to Ellie.

"All right." Ellie turned back to the screen. The Mystery Man was whistling and looking at his watch, making it very clear that he was bored with waiting for her answer.

"Yes!" she said. "OK!"

"Yes, OK... what?" said the Mystery Man.

"Yes, OK, we'll have the Controller. On a free trial."

The Mystery Man shook his head slowly.

"Yes, OK, we'll have the Controller on a free trial... what?"

"Hey. Morris."

From just behind the door now.

"Yes, Isla?"

"Let's go back in there. I wanna see the video-game stuff those Stone twins were looking at…"

Fred turned to Ellie. She didn't seem to hear them.

"Do I *really* have to say please to a computer?" she said.

"YES, YOU DO! PLEASE!" said Fred.

She sighed and turned back towards the screen. "Yes, OK, we'll have the Controller on a free trial… *PLEASE.*"

The Mystery Man nodded, as if to say, *That's right at last* – clicked his fingers and vanished.

Ellie frowned. "Is that it? I don't have to spend ages filling out forms and pretending to be over eightee—"

Fred slammed the laptop shut and, swerving past Isla and Morris who were coming through the door, pulled Ellie out of the computer room.

CHAPTER 9
The package

Ellie was still fretting on the way home, all the way to their front door.

"But why didn't we have to pay for it? How's it going to get here? *When* is it going to get he—"

"Ellie!"

The door opened. Janine was standing there with Margaret Scratcher in one hand and, in the other, a package.

"What's this?" she said.

"I don't know," said Ellie, going into the house.

"It's a *package*, Ellie. Something you've obviously bought off the internet. How many times must I tell you I don't want you buying stuff online without asking us...?"

Ellie frowned. "I haven't actually *bought* anything off the internet..."

"Well, it's addressed to Ellie Stone."

"Hang on, Mum," said Fred, picking up some ripped-open cardboard, "it's addressed to you."

"No, that was something else that arrived at the same time. Which I did order. That." She pointed to a pile of mail – there was always a pile of mail in the Stones' hallway, some of which seemed to stay unopened for years – on top of which was a polythene pack, labelled 'FATANX'.

"What's that?" said Ellie.

"It's a corset," said Janine. "Basically."

"What's a corset?" said Fred.

"Don't you remember?" said Ellie. "We did them at school, when they were teaching us about the Victorians. They're these horrible tight bits of underwear that women used to have to wear to look slimmer and force their waists to be really tiny. Mum, you shouldn't have got one of those, they're really bad, and besides you don't need it—"

"It's not for me, it's for your father," said Janine.

"Oh," said Ellie.

"Anyway, stop changing the subject. Where did you get *this* from?" She held up the unopened package, the one addressed to Ellie.

"I don't know," said Ellie. "I haven't ordered anything. Has it got the address where it was sent from on it somewhere?"

Janine squinted at the package. Then, as if it might help, she extended the arm holding Margaret Scratcher towards it, as if she – Margaret – might be able to spot something she – Janine – could not.

"No. That's odd. There's no other writing on it."

"Anyway, Mum, can I have it?"

Janine looked uncertain, but suddenly Margaret Scratcher made her move.

Janine Stone was always, day and night, holding Margaret Scratcher. Ellie and Fred would sometimes wonder how the cat ever went for a wee or a poo, since, apart from when feeding, their mother always seemed to have her lying across her left arm. What wasn't clear was how Margaret felt about it. Well. It was sometimes clear. Sometimes, Margaret would clearly think, *What am I doing constantly hanging about on this woman's arm?* and make a bolt for it. Up Janine's arm and round the back of her head.

But Fred and Ellie's mum was not one to give up easily. She would grab Margaret and hold her at arm's length while her paws wheeled about like a furry electric fan with claws, until finally the cat calmed down, gave up and went back to sleeping on her arm.

This is exactly what had just happened. There was a lot of yowling and Janine shouting: "Margaret! Margaret! Margaret! Margaret!" – higher and higher each time – and then she dropped the package.

It was Fred who caught it, but Ellie who said: "Great! Let's go to the playroom!"

CHAPTER 10
Pair with Controller

The playroom in the Stones' house was about as much of a playroom as the computer room at the school was a computer room. It was basically the spare room. It had a bed in it that Fred and Ellie's grandparents used when they came to stay, a threadbare carpet and a basket for Margaret Scratcher to sleep in.[8]

---

[8] Which she never did since Janine always made sure the cat slept on her and Eric's bed. And was always upset that, in the morning, Margaret Scratcher would not be snuggled in with her, but on top of Eric's head. "It's the smell of bacon," she would tell herself.

But the playroom did also have a TV screen on the wall, and so had become the room in which Fred and Ellie played video games, normally sitting on the floor, or sometimes – when it hadn't just been slept in by their grandparents and could be a little... musty – on the bed.

As soon as they got in there, Ellie tore at the package, ripping it to pieces.

"It can't be, can it? I mean... it just can't!" she was saying.

"No, it can't," said Fred. "It's not possible."

But it was. Ellie reached into the box and took out... the Controller. The black one with the blue lines and the buttons like jewels. Exactly the one that they had seen on the computer only half an hour earlier.

"I don't understand it," said Ellie. "How can it have got here so quickly...?"

"I don't know," said Fred.

Ellie turned the Controller over, looking for clues. But on the back there was no company name, no writing: just a shiny metal plate underneath which, she assumed, were the batteries. A *very* shiny metal plate: she could see her face in it. This distracted her for a minute. Ellie never really thought about her appearance most of the time. She just looked how she looked.

But, since Isla had said that thing about *girls with glasses*, Ellie had started wondering about it. If maybe she should try to look a bit different. If, maybe, the glasses and the braces and stuff – the whole looking just like her brother thing – if maybe it was a bit—

"But… how does it feel? In your hands?" said Fred, breaking her train of thought.

Ellie held the Controller and moved it slowly up and down in her hands, as if weighing it. She flicked her thumb on to the control stick, rolling it around. Her fingers roamed searchingly over the front buttons.

She looked up at her brother. She was smiling. She may even, although Fred wasn't sure, have had the beginnings of a tear in her eye.

"Perfect. It feels perfect."

Fred smiled back, pleased that his sister was pleased.

"Is that how it comes?" he said. "Just straight out of the package? No instructions?"

Ellie looked back in the box. She scrunched around some paper.

"No. Just… this…" she said. She took out a black bracelet, also with a blue glowing line around it. There was a label attached to it, which read:

PLEASE PAIR WITH THE CONTROLLER

"What does that mean?" said Fred.

"I don't know," said Ellie.

"Well, you're the video-game expert," he said.

Ellie shrugged and put the bracelet on. It fitted well on her wrist. But, when she picked up the Controller again, it knocked against it, disturbing her sense of perfection.

She tried flicking it further down her arm, but every time she put her hands back on to the Controller the bracelet slid down and got in the way.

"Aargh!" she said, handing it to her brother. "Can you hold this, till we find out how it works?"

"OK," said Fred, sliding the bracelet round his wrist. He quite liked the look of it. It made him feel like a pop star. *Perhaps I should get another one*, he thought, *to wear on the other wrist. With spikes...*

Meanwhile, Ellie was trying to make the Controller work. She switched on the console. The TV screen came on, with all the graphics on it.

But the graphics didn't seem to know that the Controller was in the room. She pressed the main button on it, the one with a picture that looked like someone dancing; she pressed all the other buttons, the ones that looked like jewels; she even shook it, like a maraca. Nothing. Both the console and the screen seemed unable to pick up the Controller.

"What are you meant to do?!" she said.

"I don't know," said Fred.

"Are you meant to charge it up?"

"I don't know."

"Are you meant to set it up with a computer?"

"I don't know."

"How do you even *switch it on*?"

"I don't know."

"*Urrrrrgggggggghhhhhhhhh!!!!!!*" said Ellie. And lifted the Controller up in the air, with both hands, as if she was going to smash it down hard on the floor of the playroom. Fred, who hated the thought of anything breaking – and who was still, as he always had been as a toddler, a little scared of loud noises – held up his hands to stop her.

And it was then that the Controller – and Fred's bracelet – lit up.

CHAPTER 11
Prepare yourself

"Uh-oh," said Ellie.

"Oh-uh," said Fred.

Her hands were in the air. So were his. The Controller and the bracelet were close to each other. Something about this closeness must have had an effect because the blue lines on the Controller were suddenly pulsing. As was the blue light on the bracelet.

"That's... good... isn't it?" said Ellie, bringing the

Controller back down again.

"Yes," said Fred. "I think so."

Ellie pointed the Controller at the screen. The game options were up: *FIFA. Street Fighter. Super Mario. Minecraft.* But the device wasn't lighting up any of the boxes with the game icons in them. She held it closer, towards *Mario.* In desperation, she started pressing the buttons and toggling the control stick randomly.

"It's not working, Fred! It's still not working!"

"What's happening?" shouted Fred suddenly. "Ellie? What's happening?"

Ellie looked round. Fred was crouching on the window ledge. Luckily, the window was shut.

"What are you doing there?"

"I don't know," said Fred.

"You don't know what you're doing there?"

"Well, I'm crouching. What I mean is I don't know how I *got* here."

"Fred. Don't be stupid! You must have climbed up there…"

"I didn't climb. I jumped!"

"What do you mean you jumped? In one go?"

"Yes."

"Without falling off?"

"Yes."

Ellie stared at him. The window was about a metre off the ground.

"Are you sure?"

"Ellie. I was just standing there. Next to you. You were looking at the screen. And fiddling with the Controller. Next thing I knew I'd jumped up here."

Ellie stared at him some more. Then she noticed something: the blue light on the Controller in her hands, and the blue light on the bracelet around her brother's wrist, were pulsing in time with each other. *Perfectly* in time with each other.

So she said, "Say that again."

"Next thing I knew I had ju—"

"No – before that."

Fred frowned. "You were looking at the screen…?"

"No, in between that and the jumping bit…"

Fred frowned again. "You were… fiddling with the Controller…?"

Ellie nodded slowly. "I was, wasn't I…" she said and not like it was a question. She nodded again. "Fred? Can you just… prepare yourself? I'd like to try something."

"Prepare myself? In what way…?"

"I dunno. Just… make ready."

Fred had no idea what that meant. But he took a deep breath and said: "OK."

CHAPTER 12
WWWWOOOAARGGGH!

Ellie was the more confident twin. She'd always been the one to make decisions, the one who knew what was what. She was more grown-up, more likely to understand stuff that Fred didn't, quite, yet.

But although she was acting like she knew what was what here – taking control, telling Fred to make ready, all that – she didn't *really* understand what was going on. She didn't really think that Fred had got up on to the window ledge in the way her brain was telling her he must have. And she didn't really think anything was going to happen when she pointed the Controller back at Fred and flicked the control stick downwards, while pressing the emerald button.

But it did.

Fred's legs extended, and he jumped gracefully off the window and landed back on the floor of the playroom.

"Oh. My. God," said Ellie.

"You see!" said Fred. "That's what happened before! Only in reverse. And… *wwwwooaargggh!!!*"

Ellie, who had been smiling in amazement while Fred was speaking, had moved the control stick of the Controller in a circle.

Which had led to – or, if not, it was a really remarkable coincidence – Fred spinning round in a circle.

Then, gaining in confidence, Ellie pressed the ruby button and flicked the control stick up at the same time. Leading to Fred – while saying "*AAARRGGGHHHH!!!!!*" – jumping up in the air and doing a perfect somersault back down again.

Once he realised he was fine and hadn't broken anything, Fred, breathless and wide-eyed, said: "Ellie! What's happening?"

"You see that bracelet you're wearing?"

"Yes."

"I think it's paired with the Controller. I think it pairs... *you* with the Controller."

Now it was Fred's turn to stare. Then he laughed. "Good one, Ellie! Very funny! Now can we talk about why I've started leaping up into the air for no reas— *WWWWOOOAAARGGH!*" he said as Ellie moved the control stick upwards while pressing the gold button – making him jump up and land with a forward roll on the spare bed.

"Oh! It's musty!" he said, coming up near the pillow.

"Fred, it's really happening! You're paired with the Controller! *You* are my avatar!"

Fred nodded, finally taking this in. "Are you going to change all my clothes and hairstyle?"

"No," said Ellie. "I'm not brilliant at making my avatars look good anyway. That's *your* speciality."

"Will it work the other way round?"

"I don't know…" she said. "Shall we have a go?"

Fred nodded excitedly. He was about to take the bracelet off – and Ellie was about to hand over the Controller – when, from outside, they heard:

"*HEEEEEELLLLLLLLP!!!!*"

CHAPTER 13
7.13

The twins ran outside. Standing on the street, looking up, was Eric, holding a bacon sandwich, and Janine, not holding Margaret Scratcher. Which meant something was wrong.

"What's happened?" said Ellie.

"MARGARET! MY LITTLE MARGARET!! MY BEAUTIFUL MRS SCRATCHER!!!" Janine was screaming, in between sobs.

"What about her?" said Fred.

"She's up there," said Eric, pointing, in between munches.

The Stones, as we know, lived in a ground-floor flat. But next door to their building was a house lived in by the Whites. The Whites were perfectly fine neighbours, except at Christmas. At Christmas, the Whites transformed their house into the biggest Christmas building in the street – maybe in the whole town. Derek White, the dad, strung light bulbs all over the front; above the living-room window was a big neon Santa, laughing in a sleigh with all twelve reindeer a-flying; and in the garden stood an enormous Christmas tree, festooned with every colour of fairy light in the fairy-light spectrum.

Fred and Ellie liked it actually. But Eric didn't. Eric thought that Derek was hogging the limelight. To say nothing of how much he was hogging the street's electricity. And the thing Eric really didn't like was that Derek built all this and switched it on… at the end of *October*.

That really annoyed Eric at the best of times. "Christmas isn't for ages!" he would always grumble, looking at next-door's lights from behind the lounge curtains.

"Oh, Eric. You're only annoyed because you won't be getting the turkey and the stuffing and all the trimmings for months…" Janine would always reply.

"No, I'm not!" Eric would then always protest.

"You're right," Janine would then always continue. "It's mainly just the sausages wrapped in bacon you're thinking about…"

But none of that was happening this time. This time, Eric and Janine were both outside while Derek White and his wife, Kirsty, and his two children, Leo and Emma, waited for Derek to throw the switch and light the lights.

Which he was about to do. He was standing by

the Christmas tree holding a plugboard. But…

"Don't you *dare*, Derek White!!" said Janine. "I'll have you reported to the RSPCA!!!"

"Look, Janine," Derek replied, "I always put my Christmas lights on at 7.15 on October the 22nd. It's 7.13 now. If your cat hasn't come down in two minutes, I'm afraid I can't answer for the consequences…"

"MARGARET!! MARGARET!!" shouted Janine.

"Yes, come on now, Mrs Scratcher," said Eric more quietly and only after he'd swallowed the last bit of his sandwich.

"*Meoooowwwwwww…*"

Fred and Ellie looked up, following the sound with their eyes. A ball of white fluff was perched on top of the Christmas tree, holding on with the tips of its paws to a big silver star: a silver star which was wired up with many, many tiny lights around its five points.

"Will she be OK up there?" said Fred.

"I'm not sure," said Ellie.

"Oh please, Lord... I promise this Christmas that I'll do anything you want... if you only rescue Margaret Scratcher from this terrible fate..."

They looked round. Janine was indeed, as these words suggested, praying: something neither Fred nor Ellie had ever heard her do before, not even at Christmas. She had her eyes closed and was facing away from the tree, possibly because that was in the general direction of the nearest church, about two miles away.

"...I promise not to watch so much daytime TV... promise not to have a go at Eric so much... promise to make sure the kids don't have to eat his bacon sandwiches..."

"Fred," said Ellie. "Prepare yourself."

"What...?" said Fred. Then he realised that Ellie was still carrying the Controller. And he was still wearing the bracelet.

He didn't know what she was going to do. But, whatever it was, he didn't have a good feeling about it.

CHAPTER 14
Wheee! and wheheyheey!

"... promise that I'll look after the kids better and make sure they don't come to any harm..." Janine was saying when she suddenly stopped praying. She stopped praying because she stopped talking. She stopped talking because she was staring, mouth open, at the tree. Which her son was presently climbing up.

Well, climbing isn't exactly correct. He was going up it quickly, but he wasn't clambering: he was leaping two-footed from branch to branch. He wasn't even grabbing the higher branches with his hands. He was bounding – *springing* – from branch to branch, jumping two-footed off one and landing two-footed on the next one up.

"Blimey," said Eric.

"Isn't that dangerous?" said Kirsty White.

"I think it is," said Derek White. "What's more, I want to turn my Christmas lights on very soon and this is just distracting from the whole event. Could you control your cat – and son – please?!"

"Ellie," said Janine, ignoring him. "How long has Fred been able to do… that?"

But Ellie didn't answer. To Janine's surprise, her daughter was just playing with that new video-game controller that had arrived today. Frantically playing with it, like there was a screen in front of her, which there wasn't. Obviously. Because they were outside next-door's front garden. Janine made a note to herself to have a word with Ellie at some point about this video-game obsession – she hadn't realised it had got to the point where Ellie was *pretending* to play them.

But Janine didn't think about that for very long because Fred was moving so fast he had nearly got to the top of the tree.

Ellie, meanwhile, was concentrating very hard. It was one thing to control her brother's movements in the playroom, to make him jump up and down on to the window. It was quite another to make him leap all the way up a six-metre-high tree.

But Ellie was, as we know, very, very good at video games. So, even though Fred was quite frightened, every time he jumped and landed on a new branch, he (and she) got a little more confident about what they were doing. In fact, he started to really enjoy it.

"*Wheee!*" he said. "*Wheheyheey!*"

"Is he saying… *wheee!* and *wheheyheey!?*" said Derek.

"Yes," said Eric, dumbfounded.

"Eric," said Janine. "We should tell him to come down…"

"Yes," said Eric. "Fred! Come down!"

"*After* he's got the cat, Eric!!" she said.

"Oh," said Eric.

Someone who was even more confused about what was happening than the grown-ups was Margaret Scratcher. That confusion was, in fact, quite useful because it meant that Margaret just stayed stock-still, watching in amazement as Fred came closer and closer.

Finally, Fred neared the top of the tree. He reached out a hand towards the cat.

"Hello, Margaret…" he whispered. "Come on, Margaret. Come down with me. Come to me."

Margaret Scratcher stared at him with big cat

eyes. Then she turned away, in order to have a very important and absolutely-necessary-at-this-point-in-time side wash. Lick! Lick! Lick! she went. Fred reached out his other hand and Margaret Scratcher suddenly stopped her wash, hissed and jumped off the tree, towards the living room. She landed on one of Santa's reindeer – Rudolf – and then from there, with a single leap, she moved to the Whites' roof.

"MARGARET!" shouted Janine.

"Oh dearie me," said Eric.

"One *minute*," said Derek. "You've got one minute before these lights go on..."

"But it's our son up there now!!!" said Eric.

"Rules is rules," said Derek.

Fred looked down at Ellie. Ellie had her hand on the Controller, one finger poised over the buttons. She nodded at him and mouthed the words: *Go for it – I'll make sure you don't fall.*

So Fred – because the twins, as we know, were able to lip-read each other at some distance – nodded back. He crouched down. And Ellie's fingers flew.

CHAPTER 15
Countdown

O ff the tree Fred went in a – possibly showy – triple somersault. He landed on Santa's above-the-living-room-window sleigh, skated along the top edge and then swung round the antlers of one of the reindeer – Donner, or possibly Blitzen – into the air, spinning like a top.

"OH MY!!!" screamed Eric and Janine. They ran underneath where he was, in the hope of catching him.

"It's OK, Mum and Dad!!!" Fred shouted back, although he was spinning so fast it was difficult to hear him – as soon as his mouth was the right way round, it was the wrong way round. If you see what I mean. He spun in a graceful arc on to the edge of the roof, putting one foot out to leap again, and again, across the tiles.

"What did he say?" said Eric.

"He said it was OK. And it will be," said Ellie.

"How do you know?!" said Janine. "All *you're* doing is madly practising your video-game technique!!!"

Ellie carried on working the Controller. The cat had sped off across the roof. Fred leapt over her in a single bound and landed in front of her.

Margaret reacted badly – possibly because she was no longer able to recognise this jumping, leaping person as Fred. Possibly she thought: *It's a kangaroo crossed with a monkey!* Which is understandably frightening for a cat.

She furred up like cats do, let out a long yowl and dug her claws into the roof. This wouldn't have been so worrying were it not for the large number of wires under her paws at that particular moment.

"Time's running out, Stones!" said Derek White, who seemed to have become a little crazed by it all.

"You can't switch the lights on now, Derek!" said Eric.

"My cat's up there!" said Janine.

"And our son!" said Eric.

"Yes!" she said. "Him too!"

"Come on, family," said Derek. "Time for the traditional countdown... Ten!"

The other Whites – Kirsty, Leo and Emma – looked a bit uncertain: but it's hard when a countdown starts not to join in. Especially when it's Christmas (even in October).

"Nine!" they all said.

Eric and Janine stared at each other, distraught.

Then Eric said: "Ellie!"

"Eight!"

"Ellie! You're his older twin! He always does what you tell him!"

"Yes! Tell him to come down! With Margaret Scratcher!"

"Seven… Six… Five…"

Ellie looked at her parents. Then she squinted up at the roof. Fred was approaching the cat. But Margaret Scratcher was digging her claws in. This would require something special.

"Four… Three…"

"ELLIE!!" said Eric and Janine Stone together. "DO SOMETHING!!"

"I'M DOING SOMETHING!!!" said Ellie.

She put her fingers on the right and left front bumpers of the Controller, clicking them together, while pressing down with her thumb on the diamond button and toggling the control stick from side to side.

She looked up.

Fred had leapt up again. But this time his body revolved upside down, like he was doing a cartwheel in the air. It was a trick move, which Ellie knew and most people didn't. Margaret Scratcher certainly didn't because for a second she just watched, astonished, forgetting to ruffle up her fur or growl or, most importantly, dig her claws into the wires.

Which allowed Fred, as he came down on the far side of his flying cartwheel, to grab the cat and lift her off the roof...

"Two..."

...then bounce off the guttering, fly a few metres over the garden, stick an arm out to swing round a branch of the Christmas tree and come down gracefully...

"One!!!!"

A blaze of lights (and a tinny chorus of *Jingle Bells*

from a connected iPod in the house) accompanied Fred as he landed, feet together, in front of Eric and Janine, who were staring, open-mouthed.

Fred held out Margaret Scratcher.

"Happy Christmas, Mum," he said.

CHAPTER 16
Have we got any bacon?

As soon as they were back in their own house, Fred and Ellie had a brother-sister conference in the playroom. First item on the agenda: should they tell their mum and dad what was really going on?

"I don't think so," whispered Ellie. She was whispering as the playroom was next door to the living room, where her parents were. "They wouldn't believe it anyway. And, if they did, they'd take the

Controller away and..."

"Try and sell it?" said Fred.

"Well, I was going to say give it to some scientists for tests or something, but..." and here she opened the door a little and looked at Janine and Eric, who, despite the fact that their son (and cat) had both been in danger of their lives two minutes earlier, were now settling down in front of *Cash in the Attic*, "...yes, probably."

"But what shall we tell them about what happened out there?"

Ellie thought. "We'll just have to make something up."

Fred nodded. Ellie opened the door and they walked into the living room.

"Fred!" said Janine, not taking her eyes off the screen. "That was amazing!"

"Yes," said Eric. "Amazing. Have we got any bacon?"

"Actually," said Ellie to Fred, "let's not bother."

They went back into the playroom.

"So… what *was* happening?" said Fred as soon as the door was shut.

"I don't know. I was controlling you…"

"I know that. But how?"

"I've no idea."

Fred thought about it for a while. "What game was I being?"

This might sound like a strange question, but Ellie knew what he meant. "*Super Mario.*"

Fred nodded. "That's why I was good at jumping and landing…"

"Yes," said Ellie.

"How do you know? Which game it is?"

Ellie shrugged. "That's the one I was thinking about. While I was operating the Controller…"

Fred nodded once more. "Do you think… you might be able to think about other games… in other places…?"

Ellie again knew what he meant. She looked at him and smiled.

CHAPTER 17
Good behaviour

"**S**o this month's star for Most Well-behaved Pupil... Well! You're not going to believe this, Bracket Wood!"

Everyone in the assembly hall at Bracket Wood raised their eyes to heaven. Because the same thing happened every month.

"Yes! It's a tie: between the twins from 6D – Isla and Morris Fawcett!!"

Mr Fawcett – if you'll remember, *Headmaster*

Mr Fawcett – finished his speech and started applauding. His applause was very gradually – and never entirely wholeheartedly – taken up by the rest of the school.

Meanwhile, Isla and Morris rose from their seats and came up to the podium, where their father – who never acknowledged he *was* their father at school – stood, beaming with pride.

"Well done, Isla! Well done, Morris!" he said.

"Thank you, Mr Fawcett!" they said, also pretending he wasn't their dad.

"It's your fifteenth star for good behaviour!" said Mr Fawcett. "I really don't know how you manage it!"

"We just love being polite and nice and doing our best to make everyone else at school have a good day!" said Isla.

"And *not* bully them…" said Morris.

"No…" said Isla, looking a bit annoyed. "That's right."

"Good!" said Mr Fawcett. "Let's have another round of applause for Isla and Morris!"

And, once again, he started clapping. And, once

again, the rest of the assembly hall joined in, very reluctantly.

Later that morning, at break-time, there was a big football match in the playground. All the Year Six boys, a few of the girls and some of the Year Fives were playing. It was fast and furious, which is an old-fashioned phrase, but, in this case, true: everyone was running and pushing and jumping and shouting and trying to score as fast and furiously as they could.

Fred was running down the right wing, chasing a loose ball. He had never actually scored a goal at school, even in the playground. But he could run fast and most of the players were on the other side of the pitch. If he got to the ball, and kicked it as hard as he could, he had a chance of a goal this time, he was sure.

Or he did until, about a metre away from the ball,

and with his right foot already drawn back to kick it, he fell – tumbled over in fact – head over heels down on to the asphalt. "Ow!"

"Well, well, well!" said a voice behind him. Fred looked up to see the ball being taken away by a huge mob of children. "You really must learn to do your shoelaces up, Stone…"

Fred looked down at his trainers. His shoelaces were done up. They had Ellie's triple knot on them, which of course might have been a problem if he had actually got to kick the ball.

"Yeah. *Stone*…" said another voice. A deeper – but more hesitant – voice.

Fred got up, brushed off the two leaves that had got stuck to his top and turned round.

"Hello, Isla. Hello, Morris."

"Hello, Fred."

"Don't say that, Morris."

"Why not?"

"Because it's too friendly. *Hello, Fred.* It's not very on-message for us, as bullies."

"Oh, OK, Isla. Sorry."

"You tripped me up, didn't you?" said Fred.

"Yes, I did," said Morris.

Isla sighed. "Again, Morris, you're not supposed to say that."

"Oh. What should I say?"

"I dunno! Something like…" And here Isla lowered her voice, to sound more like a boy, "*I don't think I did, Stone. Yes, my leg may have been sticking out slightly from the sidelines. But I think you ran into it.*"

"Oh, I see." Morris turned to Fred. "I don't think I did, Stone. Yes, my leg—"

"Oh, it's too late now, Morris!"

"I think you should give that good-behaviour star away!" someone else interrupted. Ellie appeared from behind the goal, holding her bag.

Morris and Isla both frowned. Morris, it was true,

had been holding their joint Most Well-behaved Pupil star throughout this altercation. He had even been holding it when he'd stuck his leg out to trip Fred up. But he looked now as if he'd forgotten it was there.

"Give it away?" said Morris. "Who to?"

"I don't know…" said Ellie. "To someone who really deserves it! Who's really nice! Like…" She looked around the playground and caught the eye of someone standing by the climbing frame, in the school's (slightly dodgy-looking) play area. He seemed to be watching her. But he probably wasn't; he was probably just looking over her head. Ellie wasn't sure whether she should say his name, but then she did anyway.

"…Rashid… I suppose."

"*OooooOOOOooooo!*" said Isla and Morris.

"Can you stop doing that, please?"

"Rashid and Ellie sitting in a tree," sang Morris.

"K... I... S... Y... um... W? B...?"

There was a long pause.

"...G."

"Yeah, like *that's* gonna happen!" said Isla. "Ever! To a girl who wears *glasses* and *braces* and *pigtails* and *dresses like she's still in Year—*"

"All right then!" cried Ellie, very embarrassed. "You should give it *back*! To the headmaster! Your *dad*. Perhaps with an explanation that you don't deserve it and to make sure it goes to someone who does next time."

"Oh right..." said Isla. "And are you – and your *brother*," she said this as if it was an insult – "going to make us?"

"Yeah, make us?" said Morris.

A small crowd had now gathered. Even the football match had paused, as more and more children started looking over nervously. Stirling and Scarlet even stopped what they were doing –

discussing which app on the phones they didn't own was best for Photoshopping – and looked over.

"Well," said Fred, "if we have to."

Isla looked to Morris; Morris looked to Isla. They shook their heads and tutted. Isla gave her brother a nod and Morris moved forward, rolling up his sleeves.

"How long did it take you to rehearse *that* series of moves?" said Ellie.

"A week. I kept on getting it wrong. Rolling up my sleeves and *then* tutting..."

"Shut up, Morris!!" said Isla. "Hang on, where's Fred?"

Morris stopped. He looked around. "Yeah. Where's Fred?"

"Here!" said a voice behind them.

They turned round and frowned.

"How did you get there...?" said Isla.

A glance passed between Fred and Ellie. Ellie

had opened her school bag and taken out: the Controller. But she had a casual look on her face, like the device was just there because she liked holding it, or because she'd brought it in for show-and-tell, or something.

And not because, in fact, she was very carefully thinking about *Street Fighter* as she flicked the control stick upwards, and pressed the silver and gold buttons at the same time.

CHAPTER 18
I'MGONNAKILLYOUUUUUUUU!!

Fred leapt into the air. Isla and Morris were not expecting this. But what they were really not expecting – this was very clear from their faces, or more specifically their mouths, which, as they looked up, were wide open – was how *high* he leapt into the air. It was about two or three metres, from a standing jump.

As he leapt, Fred bent one knee forward into a V-shape and then spun round, before landing to face them again, his right fist extended and his left held back: an attack stance.

There was a pause. Isla and Morris glanced at each other. Obviously, they were taken aback. But everybody was watching. Years of bullying were at stake. So Morris shrugged his shoulders and went to punch Fred.

Both the Fawcett twins were tall for their age. This had helped, obviously, in ruling Bracket Wood since Year One. But it had a drawback here as Morris's move forward and punch were suddenly revealed as very *slow*. Or at least they *looked* very slow, once you compared them to how fast Fred moved.

Before Morris got near him, Fred ducked, crouching down. Then, as Morris raised his arm, Fred swung one leg swiftly in a circle, scything him to the ground.

"*Oof!*" said Morris as his chin hit the asphalt, which luckily was that soft stuff that most playgrounds have now. Fred stood up and snapped back into attack position.

Morris got up, rubbing his chin. He looked at Fred warily. Not sure quite what to do, he decided to copy Fred's stance. This took a little while as at first he got his hands the wrong way round, and there was quite a lot of Morris saying to himself, "No… hang on a minute… left is this one… no, that one… OK, that's it. Oh no, it isn't…" before finally managing to stand opposite Fred, mirroring him.

He then dropped the attack stance and just ran at Fred, with both his arms above his head, going "I'MGONNAKILLYOUUUUUUUU!!"

Fred dodged out of the way. Morris ran past him into the school wall.

"*Oof!*" he said and fell down again.

He stayed down for a little while this time and Fred was wondering whether perhaps it was all over when suddenly he felt a sharp pain on his arm. He looked down to see Isla's hands twisting his skin in opposite directions to create the classic Chinese burn.

An audible gasp could be heard from the watching crowd because Isla hardly ever got involved in any actual fighting. She was the thinker, the evil genius, the psychotic but brilliant villain, and it was Morris, the henchman, who did her dirty work. But Morris was lying on the ground, just behind the hopscotch squares, going, *"Urggghh…"* so clearly this was a special case.

Isla was good at Chinese burns actually and, if she very occasionally did get involved in a fight, they were always what she liked to do. She saw it as the Thinking Bully's Move, slow and deliberate, a type of torture that was almost a piece of art. Her hands would grip tightly, closely, twisting the arm of her victim in a precise way to create the maximum amount of pain.

However, gripping this particular arm tightly turned out to be not such a good idea. Because, when Ellie saw what had happened, she pressed down the emerald button and rotated the control stick quickly in a circle, making Fred's arm rise in the air and then move round and round at top speed like the blade of a helicopter.

It was an amazing sight: Isla Fawcett circling in the air around Fred's head like a swingball. She screamed very loudly and clung on to his arm very, very tightly, which was probably the right thing to do because, if she'd let go, she would have ended up on the school roof.

The crowd of kids, excited now by the thought that Fred might actually win this fight, cheered, almost as if that's exactly what they wanted to happen.

What *actually* happened, though, was that Morris got up from the ground and, slightly dazed, turned back to try and carry on fighting Fred; at which point he was hit in the face by his own sister's flailing legs.

"*Oof!*" he said once more, as this time the back of his head hit the ground. Luckily, there was very little brain in there to be damaged.

Ellie pressed some more buttons. Fred's arm stopped circling and dropped Isla, who stood up for about half a second, before twirling to the ground with dizziness. *Bang!* She landed next to Morris.

The crowd cheered again.

Isla and Morris struggled up, holding on to each other. They were clearly frightened, but Isla said: "Listen, Morris. There are two of us. And one of him."

"Yes," said Morris, rubbing the back of his head. "So... that means we outnumber him by at least three."

"Oh God," said Isla. "The point is there's safety in numbers. Or rather..." And here she turned to face

Fred, who'd gone back to his attack stance, "there's victory in numbers!!"

Morris understood that at least. Together, with their faces set to full Bully Mode – eyes narrow, forehead low, teeth gritted – they charged at Fred.

Ellie waited until they were both near him, on either side, with their fists flying. Then her fingers darted across the Controller...

...and Fred crouched again. He stuck both hands out and placed a palm on each bully's stomach, stopping them in their tracks. Then he lifted them up in the air, until they were both horizontal. Weirdly, their fists kept moving, so it looked a bit like they were in a swimming race. Except without any water. And in a playground. With their clothes on.

"What's going on, Isla?!" screamed Morris.

"I don't know, Morris!" shrieked Isla.

Which was the last thing either of them said before Fred started *juggling* with them.

CHAPTER 19
My turn

"**W**ow!"

"Wow!"

"Wow wow wow wow wow!!!!"

Fred and Ellie were back in the playroom, discussing the events of the day.

"*Wowwwwwwwwwwww!!!!*" Fred was saying.

"Thank God you put them down just before Mr Fawcett came out!"

"Yes! I saw him coming through the door – in

between Isla's face and Morris's face as they went past – so that's when I decided to catch them."

Mr Fawcett, it has to be said, had been a bit confused. He made a point, generally, of not over-acknowledging Isla and Morris in the playground. Sometimes, he would sneak in a wave and once he'd been seen secretly trying to blow Morris a kiss, but mainly he liked to pretend that they were just like any other pupils at Bracket Wood. So he didn't quite know what to do when, on emerging from inside the school, he saw both of his children running away as fast as they could from a crowd of other cheering children around Fred Stone.[9]

He chose, in the end, just to nod to himself three times and then go back inside the school, as if nothing was wrong. Because otherwise he would

---

[9] Well. As fast as they could after being juggled: which wasn't that fast as it involved them falling over dizzily, then getting up again, then running a bit more, then falling over again, then getting up again, etc. etc. This made it all the more confusing for Mr Fawcett.

have had to go over to Isla and Morris and ask them what *was* wrong; and if something *was* wrong then he might have had to hug them to make them feel better; and then he might have ended up bursting into tears himself and all that wouldn't really work with the *"I-treat-my-children-just-like-any-other-pupils"* thing.

"This is amazing!" said Fred, holding his arm up and pointing at his bracelet. "I want to do other stuff!"

"Yes. But—"

"Like football!"

"Yes. But—"

"Because if you can control me like *Super Mario* and *Street Fighter* then you can control me like someone off *FIFA!*"

"Yes. But—"

"And then I can get into the school team! And hey! Never mind the school team, I could—"

"FRED!!!" shouted Ellie.

Fred stopped talking. She had also put her hand up to his face.

"What?" he said.

"What about *me*?" said Ellie.

Fred frowned. "What about you?"

"When is it *my* turn?"

"Your turn to what?"

Ellie looked at him like he was mad, like it was obvious. "To get to be controlled! To get to be the one who becomes…"

She struggled for the word for a little while. Then, as if it was a slightly embarrassing word, slightly babyish, but did sum up best how she felt, said, "…magic."

"Oh…" said Fred. "But…"

"What?"

"Well… you're the one who's better at video games. You're the one who's great with the Controller."

Ellie opened her mouth to speak, but then shut it

again: she knew this was true.

"But I don't mind," said Fred. "I can try. What game do you want to be?"

Ellie paused. What game *did* she want to be?

There was a knock on the door and in came Eric. Well, actually, he didn't come in since the door to the playroom tended to stick on the carpet without opening fully, which meant that while there was easily enough room for Fred and Ellie to come and go, Eric had to squeeze through. On this particular occasion, he started to do that and got stuck.

"OH GOD," he said. "JANINE! JANINE?! CAN YOU PUSH ME?"

"WHAT?"

"PUSH ME! I'VE GOT STUCK IN THE DOOR!"

"PUSH YOURSELF!"

"*PUSH YOURSELF?* WHAT DOES THAT EVEN MEAN?"

"Dad…" said Fred, "what is it?"

Eric sighed and managed, with some discomfort, to force his right arm in between the side of his torso and the door frame. He was holding an envelope. His hand waggled with the effort.

"This got dropped through the door. For you."

Fred took it from his dad.

"By the way, you two," said Eric, "have you done a Christmas list yet?"

"Don't worry, Dad, we will," said Ellie, not really looking at him: that envelope had piqued her interest.

"Well, OK, but better get on with it," he replied. "Next-door's lights keep on reminding me at least!"

Getting no response to this, Eric, with some more effort, and a loud *pop!*, reversed back out of the door.

Fred, meanwhile, had opened the envelope.

"What is it?" said Ellie.

"It's an invitation. To Rashid's birthday party. In two weeks."

"Oh, OK…" said Ellie, looking down. "Are you

going to go?"

"Yeah! I didn't think he liked me very much! He's cool!"

"Yes," said Ellie, still looking down.

"Oh, look, he's written something in it... *Hey, Fred, that was amazing in the playground today. Hope you can come.*"

"Oh..." said Ellie, *still* looking down.

"*And bring Ellie.*"

Ellie looked up.

"Really?"

Fred turned the invite round to show her. Ellie went red. But smiled. "Um. That's... nice."

"Yes!"

Ellie carried on looking at the invitation. Then her face clouded over. "Still. He's probably just being polite..." she said.

Fred thought about this. Rashid was definitely a very polite boy. But surely that was a good thing?

"I don't think I want to go, really," Ellie continued.

This confused Fred even more. "Why not?"

Ellie sighed. "I just think it won't be a party for… girls with glasses and braces and pigtails, who dress like they're still in Year One."

Fred frowned. "Why are you saying the stuff Isla always says about you when she's being horrible?"

"I don't know," said Ellie. Then, for a moment, she looked very sad, before adding: "Maybe because she's right."

Fred didn't completely understand what it was that was making his sister so upset. He also didn't understand why she would say she didn't want to go to Rashid's party, when he knew that she definitely did want to. But he knew it was all to do with how Isla had made Ellie feel about what she looked like. Which gave him an idea.

"Ellie," he said. "Put the bracelet on."

CHAPTER 20
Ellie Premium Edition

"Is this really going to work?" said Ellie. She was standing in front of the playroom mirror. Fred was next to her, holding the Controller.

"I don't know," said Fred.

"Will it hurt?"

Fred paused a second before answering. "No. I don't think so. None of that jumping about has hurt me so far."

"OK. Go for it."

"Where do you want to start? Who do you want to look like?"

Ellie thought for a moment. "I don't know. I guess… what do they make girls look like in video games?"

Fred thought. "Same as they do in cartoons and films and stuff. The pretty ones all look the same. Do you want to look like that?"

Ellie shrugged, nervously. "We could see, I suppose. What it was like…"

Fred nodded. He looked down at the Controller. Not sure what to press, he went first for a long press of the amber button.

Ellie's face went red as a tomato, and her cheeks blew up like a hamster.

"Um… sorry," said Fred. Quickly, he tried the ruby button, while toggling the control.

Ellie's face sprouted a long white beard, and her feet became as big as clowns' feet.

"OK, maybe we should forget this…" she said,

her voice quite a lot deeper than usual.

"No, wait a minute. Let me have one more go." Fred focused on the Controller. He remembered what Ellie had said when she first started to really understand how to work the device, how she had been thinking about *Super Mario* to make him jump through the air. So this time, while pressing the buttons (diamond and silver, this time, alternately) he concentrated, and tried to call up in his mind all the images in his memory of the main girl characters in video games and cartoons and films.

He thought of Princess Peach[10] and Amy Rose[11] and Misty[12] and Princess Fiona[13] and Sam the TV reporter[14] and Joy[15] and Elsa[16] and Rapunzel[17] and Mulan and Ariel and Sleeping Beauty, all the way back to Snow White.

And Ellie's braces and glasses disappeared.

"Oh my God!" she said.

"Can you see OK?" said Fred.

"Yes!" said Ellie. "Keep going…"

Fred pressed the emerald button. Suddenly Ellie's eyes grew bigger! Much bigger! They seemed to take up loads of her face! But it was OK, because her nose had got smaller, making room for them.

"Do you like it?" said Fred.

Ellie was looking at herself in the mirror.

"I think you might be able to see the effect more if you shut your mouth," said Fred.

Ellie did so. Then looked at herself again. "Have my lips got bigger?" she said.

"Yes. And redder. And shaped like a heart."

"OK," she said. "It's weird."

"But do you like it?"

---

[10] From *Super Mario*.

[11] From *Sonic The Hedgehog*.

[12] From *Pokemon*.

[13] From *Shrek*. When she's not green.

[14] From *Cloudy With a Chance of Meatballs*. Bit of a curve ball that one.

[15] From *Inside Out*.

[16] From *Frozen*. But you knew that.

[17] OK I'm gonna stop now.

She half-nodded. "I *think* so…"

Fred took this as meaning he should carry on. So his fingers went back to the Controller's buttons.

And Ellie changed shape: she grew a few centimetres taller and simultaneously her neck became longer, her waist contracted and her shoulders expanded, so that her top half looked like an upside-down triangle. Sister and brother looked on, amazed.

"What about my…?" said Ellie, pointing to the back of her head.

"On it!" said Fred.

Fred's fingers continued to work. Ellie's pigtails vanished, and her hair… it didn't just grow, it *flowed* from her scalp in waves!

"Oh! Oh!" said Ellie, as it settled on her shoulders looking glossy and full and shiny and all the other things people said about hair in their mum's magazines. But, in the mirror, she didn't even have time to look at that properly, before her school uniform, which had instantly tailored itself to fit her new shape, started changing colour, flashing red! Black! Gold!

"What's it doing?!" said Ellie.

"Offering up suggestions, I think!" said Fred. "What colours do you want?"

"I dunno!"

Fred went for black and gold, a tiny bit like the colours a posh chocolate might be wrapped in. As he did so, Ellie's school uniform stopped looking like a school uniform at all, and more like a beautiful party dress.

He stopped pressing the buttons. Ellie looked at her

entire new self in the mirror. She shook her head with disbelief.

"What do you think?" said Fred.

"It's amazing," said Ellie. "But... do I even look like myself any more?"

Fred turned his head to the mirror, considering. "Yes," he said, after a while. "You look like Ellie but... upgraded. Ellie 2.0. Ellie Premium Edition."

Ellie took this in. It certainly *sounded* good. Although to be honest, Fred often expressed himself in video-game language. "What about when Mum and Dad see me...?" she said. "What am I going to tell them about how I look? And where I got these clothes? And—"

"God! There you are!"

Fred and Ellie turned round. Their mum was standing at the door of the playroom with her arms crossed, staring hard at the two of them.

CHAPTER 21
You're my stylist

"**W**hat have you two been doing in here?" said Janine from the doorway. "Oh, don't tell me…" She looked at the Controller in Fred's hands. "Video games. I knew it. You're addicted! Completely *addicted*! I've had to miss nearly *four minutes* of *Cash in the Attic* searching for you."

Fred and Ellie looked at each other, with deadpan expressions on their faces. They were much younger than their mother, obviously, but the irony of what she had just said was lost only on Janine Stone.

"*And* it's the Christmas celebrity edition! With Cheryl Baker! Isn't it, Eric?"

"It is, Janine," said Eric, appearing at his wife's shoulder.

"Anyway," said Janine, "tea's ready."

"Is it bacon sandwiches?" asked Eric.

"No, of course it isn't. That's a breakfast option. And besides it's not your tea, it's their tea."

"Oh, OK."

Both adults turned to leave. Fred looked to Ellie. Ellie looked to Fred. Together they shook their heads, amazed.

"Hang on a minute," said Janine, suddenly coming back through the door with a suspicious look on her face. "Ellie!"

"Er… yes, Mum?"

"Look at me," said Janine. Ellie gazed at her mum through her newly widened eyes. She tried not to look down at her new premium self.

"Ellie Stone, tell me the truth."

"Yes, Mum."

"Have you… fed Margaret Scratcher?"

Ellie frowned. Fred frowned.

"Er… no?" she said.

"I knew it!" said Janine. "You promised to feed her this afternoon and you've just been too lazy to do it! But I could tell you felt guilty about it. I could *see it in your eyes!*"

"Can't hide anything from you, Janine!" came Eric's voice from outside.

"Tell me about it, Eric!" said Janine, triumphantly turning round and leaving the room.

Ellie and Fred exchanged glances. Then they both shrugged.

"Ellie," said Fred. "I think – even though Mum and Dad didn't notice that you'd… changed – I should probably change you back. To normal. For now.

And then I can make you look like this again for the party!"

"OK," said Ellie. "Good thinking. But… hold on."

"What?" said Fred.

"You never did shoes."

"I did."

"I don't mean the clowns' shoes. I mean some proper shoes. To go with…" she gestured to herself, "all this."

"OK. What sort?"

"High heels?"

"Really? Have you ever worn high heels?"

"No. Well, I tried on a pair of Mum's once."

"Oh yes. And you fell over."

"Hmm. OK. I'll leave it to you. You're my stylist."

Fred smiled, pleased with this idea. He pressed the silver button three times and thought of shoes: fairy-tale shoes. Ellie looked down. Her normal, ordinary trainers had vanished. On her feet, perfectly fitting, were two silver slippers glittering with light. She turned to her brother gratefully.

"Yes, Cinderellie!!" he said, with a smile. "You shall go to Rashid's party!"

Part 2

UPGRADE

CHAPTER 22
Most improved

"That was incredible!"

"Not just incredible. Amazing!"

"It was the best goal I've ever seen outside of the Premier League and the World Cup!"

"What, the second goal? Or the third?"

"I thought the fourth was the best!"

"Yes, the way he caught the ball on the back of his neck, before flicking it up on to his head and knocking it down for a left-foot volley! *That* was the best one!"

Fred just smiled, listening to the things the ten other boys in the Bracket Wood First XI were saying as they carried him aloft on their shoulders off the pitch. He could hear the applause and cheering of lots of others, the rest of the school in fact, who were standing on the touchline.

"I can't believe we've finally beaten Geary Road!"

"Seven-nil!"

"They haven't even beaten *us* by that much. Ever!"

"Well, they beat us eight-nil last year…"

"Not the same."

"This means we're in the final!"

"Yes! The Bracket Wood and Surrounding Area Inter-school Winter Trophy final!"

"Yes! All because of Fred!"

"Oh no," said Fred, shaking his head in a way that:

a) wasn't believable

and

b) made the boy underneath him – who was called Prajit, and who despite being the goalie wasn't actually the biggest player on the team – wobble dangerously for a moment.

"It's a team game."

"It *is* a team game," said Mr Barrington, suddenly appearing – because Fred was on Prajit's shoulders – at eye level. Up close, his eyes looked enormous through his enormous lenses. It was, Fred thought, like having a staring match with a fish in a tracksuit.

"But there's simply no doubt that your individual performance was the best I've ever seen. I knew I was right to put you on the team, even for a game as important as this – a semi-final.

"It's a flash in the pan, some said after your trial.

Others said, *I don't understand it – he's always been rubbish before*, but I said, *No! There's a young footballer with real class, who could make a real difference to our team*, and it was because of that I decided that you were— "

"Mr Barrington?"

"Yes, Fred?"

"No, that wasn't me speaking. It was Prajit."

Mr Barrington looked down. "Ah yes, Prajit. What is it?"

"Sorry to interrupt, but I'm about to fall over."

"All right, Prajit. I've nearly finished. Surely you can hold on for another two minutes."

"Um… OK."

Mr Barrington looked back up. "What I really wanted to say, Fred, was that you are, without any doubt, the most improved player I have ever seen. How on earth have you done it?"

All the faces on the team looked up at Fred. His face, though, wasn't looking back at them. It was pointing in another direction, towards the crowd where, among all the boys and girls waving Bracket Wood scarves, he could see Ellie. She was doing a thumbs up with her right hand. In her left hand, he could see, she was still holding the Controller. When she saw him looking at her, she raised that up too, so that both her hands were in the air.

"Well…" said Fred.

"Speak up," said Mr Barrington. "I think the whole school should share in this moment. The whole school should know exactly what it was that made you suddenly such a great player. I would like you to speak up and tell us *exactly* how you did it."

CHAPTER 23
Flashback

So, before we hear Fred's answer, you need to know that some time has passed. The Whites' Christmas lights don't even look out of place any more; Eric has taken the unusual step of putting up some of his own lights outside the Stones' flat.[18] Margaret Scratcher has got considerably fluffier as it has got colder. And Fred and Ellie have been making a *lot* of use of the Controller.

---

[18] Although only along the bottom section of their front wall as, when he tried to put some lights higher up, the ladder broke.

They've used it to do their chores. (You can tidy your room *very* quickly when two flicks will propel you from the floor to the cupboard and back again. Plus, Ellie found that, if she pressed amber-plus-diamond while Fred was pointing at a pile of clothes, they just folded themselves up automatically.) They've used it to make boring car journeys more exciting (and neither Eric nor Janine even noticed that their children were doing somersaults on the roof); they even used it to spice up trick-or-treating at Halloween (it's amazing how much more frightening – and therefore how many more sweets people will give you – a cheap skeleton costume becomes when it's leaping up the side of a house).

And, of course, they used it at the November school football team trial. A lot of the other boys – and Mr Barrington – looked pained when they saw Fred approaching, all kitted up and smiling. The words "not again" and "how are the shoelaces doing?" and "oh no, he's brought his nerd sister along…" were muttered.

However, one bit of keepy-uppy, two back-heels, three drag-and-goes, four zigzags and *five goals later*, the muttering had stopped. Had turned in fact to cheering, and applause, and a first-name-on-the-sheet place in the school team for the upcoming semi-final versus Geary Road.

So now let's return to Fred and what he said to Mr. Barrington when his teacher asked him to speak up and tell everyone exactly how he did it.

CHAPTER 24
Time to shine

For a moment, Fred thought Mr Barrington must have rumbled him: that he must know that he had, in a way, cheated, because he sounded a bit like teachers did when they were being sarcastic – like Mr Barrington, having heard Fred whispering in class, was mockingly inviting him to come up and tell everyone all about the great things he had to say.

But then Fred realised, looking at the sports teacher's friendly if fishy eyes, that Mr Barrington *wasn't* being sarcastic; that he genuinely thought that it was amazing how well Fred had played and that he really wanted him to tell the rest of the school how he had done it.

Fred nodded to himself; he looked to Ellie, who still had her hands up and was also now smiling at him hopefully; and so he took a deep breath and said loudly, making sure everyone could hear him: "I don't know really, Mr Barrington. I suppose I just have a talent – an amazing talent – that I was born with."

A ripple of applause greeted this.

"Talent, though, needs hard work to make it all it can be."

He saw Mr Barrington nod and heard some people in the crowd say, "Yes… very wise."

"So maybe up till now," Fred continued, "if I was really being honest with myself, I'd have to say I haven't truly been doing the hard work. But now

I have – I've finally put in the time and the sweat and practised hard. And yes, it's paid off because…"

The ripple of applause started building, and building, and building. Fred raised a fist in the air: "…now it's my time to shine!!"

The crowd erupted into a massive roar. Mr Barrington was applauding. Fred's team-mates were applauding. Even the defeated Geary Road team were applauding.

The only person who wasn't applauding – who was in fact walking away sadly – was Ellie. Fred watched her go. He wanted to call after her. He wanted to tell her that he had only said that because he didn't know what else to say. That he'd got carried away with the moment. He wanted to say sorry. But all that was quite hard to do because:

a) she was already quite far away

b) the crowd were cheering and chanting, "Fred!

Fred! Fred!" so she wouldn't have heard him above it

and

c) just as he opened his mouth to shout after her, Prajit's legs finally went and Fred toppled headlong into Mr Barrington, knocking him, and his rhino-foot-lens glasses, into the mud.

CHAPTER 25
It's bananas, Morris

Actually, not *everybody* apart from Ellie was applauding. Two other people weren't. They were following Ellie as she walked away from the pitch.

"Stone!" said a voice behind her. She turned round, heavy-hearted.

"Isla…" she said. "Not now."

"Oh, *sorry*, Ellie," said Isla Fawcett.

"Yes, sorry, Ellie," said Morris, turning away.

"Where are you going, Morris?" said Isla.

"Um… back to the match… You said sorry – so I thought we were leaving her alone…"

"She was being sarcastic," said Ellie.

"Oh. Were you?" said Morris.

"Yes," said Isla. She sighed and shook her head. "Anyway, Ellie… that's odd. That you're leaving. Didn't fancy watching your brother's moment of triumph…?"

"I'm not interested in answering your stupid questions, Isla," said Ellie.

"Another thing that's interesting is that you're always holding that Controller these days."

Ellie gulped. "Am I?"

"Yes. I noticed you were holding it – and playing with it – all through the game. And I noticed you were *also* holding it – and playing with it – all through that… incident in the playground the other week."

"Incident? Oh, you mean when my brother completely trounced your brother – and you – in a fight?"

"Hmm. That's not how I saw it."

"It's how I saw it," said Morris.

"Shut up."

"I'm surprised you could see *anything* – let alone what *I* was doing – when you were being *juggled*," said Ellie.

"Whatever," said Isla.

"Yeah, What. Ever," said Morris, doing a W with his fingers. Well, it actually looked like a shadow-puppet person doing a very bad version of a bird. "Hang on," he said. "What's the next letter? After W?"

"Never mind. Just get it," said Isla.

"Get what?" said Ellie. But this question wasn't answered. Instead, Morris, who although slow-thinking was fast-moving, ran at her and grabbed the Controller.

"Hey!" she said. "Give that back!"

Isla smirked and held out her hand. Morris passed the Controller to her.

"I said give that back!!" shouted Ellie, reaching for it. But Morris stood in her way.

"Interesting…" said Isla, holding the Controller up and turning it round. "It's very pretty, isn't it?"

"Give it back!"

Isla smiled and brought the Controller closer to her face. "You're certainly very bothered about it, aren't you? Just what *is* it about this that makes it *so* special?"

"Nothing!" shouted Ellie. "Just leave it alone!"

"Might it be something to do with the control stick…?" said Isla, circling it round. "Or this gold button here…?"

Just before Isla rotated the control stick and pressed the gold button, 200 metres away, back at the football pitch, Mr Barrington was scrambling around in the mud for his glasses. Fred was saying, "I'm so sorry, Mr Barrington, let me help you!" Everyone else was watching.

As Isla rotated the control stick and pressed the button, Fred whirled round in a very fast circle, swung back his left foot and then kicked out, in one powerful, graceful movement, sending Mr Barrington's glasses all the way to the other end of the pitch. Sending them, in fact, soaring into Geary Road's goal, although this one, to be fair, didn't count.

"Stop it! Stop doing that!" shouted Ellie.

"Why…? What's going on…?" said Isla, pressing the ruby button over and over again.

"Fred!!!" shouted Mr Barrington. Although not at him. Instead, he was peering at Prajit, who was just getting up.

"I'm so sorry, Mr Barrington!
I really am!" said Fred.

"Are you?!" said Mr
Barrington, now – following
the sound – at least
looking towards Fred.

Unfortunately, Fred
was jumping up and
down with his
hands in the air,
seeming not
to be sorry,

but rather to be celebrating.

"Yes! I am! I'm really sorry about your glasses!"

he said, leaping especially

high and punching the air.

"Well... GO AND GET THEM THEN!!" said Mr Barrington.

"I will," said Fred, just as Isla pushed the control stick to the left. Fred rushed off very fast in the opposite direction to where the glasses were. Which was good in one sense, as that *was* the direction in which Mr Barrington was mistakenly pointing.

"Hmm..." said Isla. "It's something to do with you and your twin... and the way he's suddenly got really good at everything... but I can't work out what."

She looked at Ellie, who shrugged. She looked at Morris, who shrugged. Although he did that when you asked him what type of fruit monkeys ate.

Isla tossed the Controller on the ground.

"But I will," she said, walking away.

CHAPTER 26
A kind of looking-down smile

When Isla threw the Controller away, Fred stopped running in the wrong direction for Mr Barrington's glasses. He shook his head as if to say, "What was *that* all about!!?" and turned round to go back to the changing room.

Next to the posts of their goal a grown-up was standing: a man in his mid-thirties, wearing a smart black coat, and with a kindly, curious smile on his face.

"Hello," said the man. He had a hint of a foreign accent. "I just watched you play."

"Oh," said Fred.

"You're good."

"Oh. Thank you."

"Maybe very good."

Fred nodded and gave a smile that wasn't really a proper smile, more a kind

of looking-down smile – which was what he did when he was a bit embarrassed.

The man took a card out of his pocket. He handed it to Fred.

"This is me. I might come back and watch you again in the final. Just to make sure it wasn't a one-off…" He smiled again and turned away.

Fred looked down at the card. He had to read it three times before he could believe it.

CHAPTER 27
It's a deal

"I can't believe you did that! That speech after the game! Taking all the credit!" shouted Ellie.

"What was I supposed to say? *You're very kind, but it wasn't me it was my sister magically controlling me with that video-game Controller?*" Fred shouted back.

"No! But you didn't have to be *quite* so pleased with yourself!"

"Well, I can't believe you did what *you* did! Making me kick Barrington's glasses all the way down the pitch! I could've got expelled!"

"What are you talking about?! That was Isla! I didn't do anything!"

"Well, I'm not sure I believe *you*! I think you were trying to teach me a lesson!"

"Can you two keep it down in there?! I'm trying to watch—"

Ellie and Fred stopped arguing for a second to say together, loud enough for their mother to hear through the playroom wall: "*Cash in the Attic!!* Yes, we know!"

There was a short pause. Then Janine said: "Actually, I'm watching another programme, I'll have you know."

Ellie and Fred looked at each other.

"Really?" said Ellie.

"Yes."

"What's it called?"

"*Money in the Loft*. It's a new show. Completely different."

Fred and Ellie looked at each other again. Then they burst out laughing.

"OK, OK," said Ellie. "Can we stop arguing with each other, please?"

"Yes. Please!" said Fred. "Look. I've been dying to show you something..."

"What?"

Fred took the card out from his pocket. He held it in two hands, between his thumbs and forefingers, and thrust it at his sister.

She squinted at it. *"Sven Matthias. Junior Football Scout.* Scout?"

"Not scout as in boy who wears a funny uniform and spends a lot of time in tents studying knots. Scout as in talent scout. It's someone who works for a football club finding talented young players."

"Oh! Wow! Which football club?"

Fred moved his finger away from the top corner of the card, revealing a blue badge: a lion holding a staff. Ellie's eyes widened.

"Chelsea! *Chelsea Football Club?!*"

Fred grinned at her, nodding.

"This man wants you to come and try out for Chelsea Football Club?!"

"Well," said Fred, putting the card back in his pocket, "no. He's going to come back and watch me in the final. And then decide."

"Wow. That's amazing."

"Yes. So… look, I'm sorry. About what I said after the game. But you will come to the final, won't you? And… control me? And I promise never to make a speech about how talented I am at football again. Even in a post-match interview on *Match of the Day*."

Ellie thought about this. "Will you change me back to Cinderellie?"

Fred frowned. Then his face cleared.

"Oh! I forgot! It's Rashid's party later!"

Ellie nodded shyly.

"Yes! Of course!" said Fred.

Ellie smiled and put her hand out. "It's a deal," she said.

CHAPTER 28
A shaven gorilla

The Stones were late setting off for Rashid's party. There had been a bumper edition of *Cash in the Attic* on Channel 765 + 1.

"What channel is this?" Eric had said when the fifth *Cash in the Attic* in succession had come on.

"It's the *Cash in the Attic* channel," Janine had replied.

So, when they were finally on their way, Ellie said: "Dad. Can we go a bit faster, please?"

"Yes," said Janine. "Put your foot down, Eric."

"Er… my foot is down, Janine. Right down on the accelerator to the floor."

Janine looked at her husband's feet. It was true.

"Blimey, Eric," she said. "You really are going to have to lose some weight."

Which was why, when the Stones dropped Ellie and Fred outside Rashid's front door, the party was already in full swing. Fred had just rung the doorbell when they heard, from behind them, a familiar voice.

"Well, well, well…"

"Oh no," said Ellie. She turned round. There were Isla and Morris.

Isla was in full party gear: a bright red minidress and high heels, and long dangly earrings and full red-matching-her-dress lipstick. Oh, and her hair was at its most shampoo-advert-like, glossy and falling over her face, until she tossed it back to make the "well, well, well" just that bit more dramatic.

Morris still looked like a shaven gorilla.

"You're late," said Isla.

"So are you!" said Ellie.

"Yes, but we're *fashionably* late," said Isla.

"What does that even mean?" said Ellie.

"It means that we're late," said Isla, coming closer to her, "but we look *great.*"

"Morris doesn't," said Fred.

"That's true, I don't," said Morris.

"Shut up," said Isla. "Even you, Morris, who looks like a shaven gorilla, look better than these two. Especially you, Ellie. Jeans, V-neck jumper and glasses. Like always. Couldn't you have tried wearing something nice for the party? Couldn't you have asked Mum or Dad for some fashion advice? Oh no, you couldn't, could you? Because your mum's a telly addict and your dad's fat as a house!"

"That's true, they are," said Morris.

"Shut up!" said Fred.

The front door began to open.

"Oh well," said Isla, "I suppose that just means Rashid will only have eyes for one of us. As usual."

As she finished speaking, Isla turned away from Fred and Ellie and turned her face on: which means she stopped sneering and gave a big, bright, toothy smile to the person opening the door – who was, indeed, Rashid.

"Hello, Rashid!" she said.

"Hello, Isla. Hello, Morris," said Rashid. "And hey! Fred!"

"Hi, Rashid," said Fred.

"And… who are you?" said Rashid, looking beyond Fred.

"I'm… Ellie," said Ellie. "I'm in your class at school."

"…Ellie?" said Rashid. "Wow. You look… different."

Everyone turned towards Ellie. And indeed

she did. She looked like Snow White and Princess Fiona[19] and Joy from *Inside Out* and all the other cartoon and video-game heroines rolled into one (and yet, still, somehow, like Ellie). Her hair curled softly round her face, even more like a shampoo advert than Isla's. Her dress was black and gold.

[19] Still not green.

And on her feet, shining up and reflecting the lights of the party inside, she was wearing the spangliest silver slippers.

Everyone who had turned to look at her couldn't stop staring. She looked amazing.

"When..." said Isla, who was *really* staring, "how... when... did you change your... outfit? And... everything else about you...?"

Ellie shrugged, spreading her palms, and revealing one other item of clothing: a black bracelet on her right wrist. Which Isla noticed, although she *didn't* notice Fred putting the Controller back into his coat pocket.

CHAPTER 29
Thor's hammer of bacon

"That was *amazing*! Did you *see* Isla's face? *And* everyone else's when I walked in? How everyone took more notice of me than they ever have before?"

Fred nodded, although he was starting to get a little worried about Ellie, who had been talking like this ever since they'd left the party.

"And I danced! I never dance! But I just felt like it!"

She whirled round, her hair whirling round with

her. Fred stood back against the wall of the playroom and watched her for a moment. He was happy she was happy, but he was also a bit troubled.

"OK... what about Rashid?"

Ellie stopped in her tracks. "What about him?"

"Did you talk to him?"

Ellie looked down at her hands, spreading them out, examining her fingernails, which were long and painted red. "For a little while."

"So... do you think *he* liked... your new look?"

Ellie looked up at Fred like he was mad. "Well, of course he did!"

"So what did he say?"

"He didn't *say* anything about it. He's a boy. He's eleven! But..." said Ellie, looking at herself in the mirror and posing, like celebrities do for pictures at a film premiere, with one leg pushed out and a hand on her hip, "...he *must* have done!"

"Anyway, I'd better change you back to normal now," said Fred, picking up the Controller, which was lying on the table under the TV screen.

"No!" said Ellie, still looking at herself. "I want to stay like this!"

Fred frowned. "Stay… for how long?"

"I don't know. I like it. Forever?"

"Ever?"

"Well…" said Ellie. "Yes. Why not?"

Fred looked at her. He didn't actually know the answer to that question. One thing he wanted to say was: *Because you're my twin. And, even though we're not identical, we're supposed to look, and be, similar. And now you're not looking, or being, similar. I'm not sure who you're being at the moment.*

That's what he wanted to say. But it felt a bit sad and rubbish. And besides, it was all his fault, as he'd done the changing, he'd invented Cinderellie. He was her stylist.

So instead he just looked down at the Controller. On which the blue light was doing something strange.

"What's going on?" said Fred.

"What do you mean?" said Ellie, *still* looking at herself in the mirror.

"The Controller. It's doing something weird…"

That finally made Ellie turn. She looked down at the Controller. Its blue light was flashing. Not pulsing any more. But flashing. Quickly.

She looked down at her bracelet. It was flashing too.

"What does this mean?" she said.

"I don't know," said Fred.

Ellie picked up the Controller. She shook it. She turned it upside down.

"Does it mean the power's running out?"

"It might."

"But how do we charge it up? Or change the battery?"

"I don't know. If you remember, that's what I said when you asked me that when it first arrived."

Ellie turned it round. The shiny metal plate reflected her new blonde hair and big eyes and larger lips. But there were no screws on it and no arrows: nothing to suggest that you could take it off and see batteries lined up snugly underneath.

"Well… what are we going to do?" she said.

Fred thought for a second. "We could go online and find the Mystery Man?"

"Great idea!"

They rushed into the kitchen, in search of the family laptop. It was a bugbear of Fred and Ellie's that the Stones only had one computer and that, most of the time, no one knew where it was. However, this time it was obvious: in Eric Stone's right hand, playing a YouTube clip of Jamie Oliver making a bacon sandwich.

"…now officially, a great sarnie has BROWN

sauce," Jamie was saying, "but I think ketchup with just a dash of Tabasco makes a…"

"Dad!" said Ellie. "What are you doing?"

Eric Stone looked round. In his left hand he was holding a packet of bacon as big as Thor's hammer, if indeed Thor's hammer had been made out of cured ham.

He also had four or five frying pans piled up on the stove with various bottles of condiments: brown and red sauce, mayonnaise, mustard, piccalilli and a jar of Indian pickle that no one knew the name of and everyone had been too frightened to open up until this point. He was wearing a chef's hat and a large apron straining at its back knot. It was a novelty apron that Janine had got him last Christmas, which had on the front a photograph of a man's stomach, but not Eric Stone's stomach: a model's stomach, with a six-pack.

"I'm just checking the recipe…" he said.

"The *recipe*?" said Fred. "Bacon. Bread. Sauce. That's it."

"Aaah, but you see, Jamie – he's got a whole new way with bacon, bread and sauce... Ellie, what are you doing?!"

"I'm taking the laptop away! The screen's already got splattered with bacon fat!" said Ellie, moving back towards the playroom.

"Bring that back here!"

"No!" said Ellie.

"...and if you rub the bread into the pan afterwards," said Jamie, "you get a..."

"What did he say? WHAT DID HE SAY?" shouted Eric. But it was too late. Ellie had clicked off the screen. Eric put his head in his hands. Which was a mistake as he was still holding the Thor hammer of bacon.

CHAPTER 30
Actually, it's not Skype

"It's not here!" said Ellie twenty minutes later. "I've searched everywhere!"

She had. They'd googled everything: Controller, Mystery Man, Man of Mystery, nerd-obsessed balding grown-up with little sunglasses who gets upset when you ask him questions… Nothing.

They stared at the screen. Suddenly a Skype-like sound started coming out of it. *Bing bong bing bing.*

"Oh!" said Ellie. "Maybe this is him! Maybe

he's found *us!*"

"Yes!" said Fred, accepting the call. A window opened up on the screen. There didn't appear to be anyone there, just a blank wall and an empty chair.

"Hello!" said a voice.

"Hello!" said another voice.

"Who is it?" said Ellie.

"It's us!" said the first voice as its owner – Stirling – repositioned the webcam so that he could be seen clambering up on to a chair.

"Sorry," said the second voice – Scarlet, obviously – "but sometimes we're too small for Mum's webcam." She clambered up too, smiling and waving.

"Is she there?" said Fred. "I thought you weren't allowed to use the computer unsupervised."

"She was just in here," said Scarlet. "She said we could use it to look for some Christmas pressies."

"So you're going to search for something on

Amazon?" said Ellie.

Stirling and Scarlet looked at each other and burst out laughing. "Oh dear, oh dear, oh dear!" they said.

"I think not, Grandma!" said Stirling. "The state-of-the-art site for the up-to-the-minute shopper these days is, of course..."

"Pret-a-Pick-n-Mix?" said Scarlet. "Mammamammon? Shopjock? PayUsPlease? Londis.Com? BuyStuff?"

"All fabulous, Scarlet, but the one we're going to use is..."

"Look, I don't care," said Ellie. "We've got a problem. And now you're here it strikes me that you two iBabies might be able to help us with it."

So then Fred and Ellie – after making them promise that they wouldn't tell anyone else about it ever, ever, ever – told Scarlet and Stirling all about the Controller.[20] And about how they couldn't now

---

[20] Which they were very excited by, although Stirling still thought they could have got a better one at Getmethatgadget.

make contact with the Mystery Man, or even find any reference to him anywhere on the internet.

The iBabies thought for a while. Then Scarlet said: "Maybe... maybe he only appears on the laptop at school. The old one?"

"OMG, that antique!" said Stirling. "It's *so* like our school not to have an iDesk, or a TechHammer, or a PixSonic 250. But yes, I bet Scarlet's right! It's so old maybe it was built by, like, a medieval wizard or something!"

Ellie frowned. "Isn't the internet just a big thing that's the same on all computers?" she said. "If he's on that one, he should be on this one."

"Yes," said Scarlet. "But most video-game controllers don't control people."

There was no doubt this was true. Ellie turned to Fred, with a *what do you think?* face. He did a *the iBabies might be right* shrug.

But, before they could carry on the conversation,

Scarlet and Stirling's mum and stepdad appeared behind them.

"Oy! I never said you could use that to Skype someone!" said their mum, who was blonde and had a Scottish accent.

"Yes, that is right," said their stepdad, Mr Bodzharov, who had very thick black hair, a moustache and an Eastern European accent. "I have warned you. You know I will have to punish you if you disobey your mother."

"Please don't cut our hair again like they do in the Old Country!" said Scarlet.

"What?" said Mr Bodzharov. "That is not a punishment! That is a reward! No, I meant no more pocket money."

"Actually, it's not Skype, Mother," said Stirling. "It's FaceFace, which uses a whole different system—"

Scarlet and Stirling's mum switched off the link.

Ellie and Fred laughed. And then Fred said: "So maybe, first thing Monday morning, we go to the computer room and—"

"No! I think we should go now!" said Ellie.

"Now?"

"Yes! We need to know what's happening!"

"But it's Saturday. The school will be locked up!"

Ellie nodded and held up the Controller. "I'm pretty sure this has still got enough charge to deal with that…"

The Skype – sorry, FaceFace – *bing-bong* started up again. Fred sighed. Ellie shook her head. She clicked on ACCEPT.

"Hello!" said Scarlet's voice, whispering.

"Hello!" said Stirling's voice, also whispering.

"What is it, iBabies?" said Ellie.

"We had an idea," said Scarlet, "after Mum and Mr Bodzharov went out of the room!"

"Yes, we thought that you could go to the school

over the weekend, even though it's locked up, and use the Controller to maybe…"

"Yes, we've already had that idea," said Fred. "We're going later today."

"Oh," said Scarlet.

"Oh," said Stirling.

There was a short pause.

"Can we come?" said the iBabies together.

"No," said Fred.

"No," said Ellie.

"Why not?" said Scarlet.

"Because you're iBabies," said Ellie.

"Yes. And you call your stepdad Mr Bodzharov," said Fred, clicking on END CALL.

CHAPTER 31
NO MORE QUESTIONS!

By the time they arrived at the school gates, it was getting dark. Ellie said to Fred: "Hold your hand out."

"*Minecraft?*" said Fred.

"*Minecraft,*" said Ellie. She pressed the ruby button of the Controller. Suddenly a rectangular object, made out of blocks, appeared in Fred's hand. It was brown with yellow at the end. It lit up.

"A torch!" said Fred.

"Give it here," said Ellie. She angled it towards Fred, to light up what they needed to do next. Fred held out his hand. Ellie pressed the gold button. A stone tool, like a shovel or a hoe, appeared between his fingers.

Fred immediately started digging.

Ellie moved backwards to avoid the spray of dirt and dust. But not for long as Fred had very quickly – in about six big blocks of concrete, which flew out behind him – dug a tunnel under the gates and appeared on the other side. Ellie followed him. The walls he had dug were remarkably square and neat.

She came out on the school side.

"Hold on a minute," said Fred. He vanished

back inside the tunnel. From the other side of the gates, Ellie watched as he threw each block down the hole, to fill it in.

"Don't want anyone falling down that," Fred said through the gates. "Or seeing what we've done."

"Yes, but now you're on the wrong side again."

Fred nodded. "Float me over."

Ellie tutted. But she pressed the diamond button, and moved the control stick, and next thing you know Fred was gliding into the air, as if in slow motion, up and over the school gates and down again, to land gracefully next to Ellie on the other side.

"That was fun!" he said.

"You're wasting the battery," she said.

"We don't even know if it *has* a battery."

"It's not flashing like that for nothing," said Ellie, gesturing at the Controller.

They had to dig another tunnel to get into the

building itself. Then they found that the door to the computer room was locked.

But Ellie had an idea. She clicked on the Controller and Fred held out his hands: a wooden plank appeared in them. Then another and another. Fred arranged the planks against the wall of the computer room to form another door. Which wasn't locked.

They went in. Inside, the laptop was sitting on the table, exactly where they'd left it. (Not a lot of people used the school computer room.) It was displaying its screensaver, which was a photo of a smiling Mr Fawcett at the school gates with a group of children of all different ethnic backgrounds. The twins sat down in front of it. They glanced at each other, nervously.

"If we can't find him on this one..." said Fred.

"I know," said Ellie.

She clicked on the computer. The screensaver

vanished and there, in exactly the same room as before, wearing exactly the same clothes, was the Mystery Man.

"Oh! Well! Thank the Lord!" he said. "I thought you were *never* coming back!"

"What?" said Ellie. "Do you mean you've been there the whole time?"

"Yes! You're meant to shut the computer down when you've finished using it! It's basic environmental good sense!"

"So… you've stayed sitting there for weeks to teach us a lesson about how to help save the environment?" said Ellie.

The Mystery Man, who had been looking flustered anyway, looked even more flustered. He looked Premium Edition Flustered.

"I've told you before, you're not allowed to ask me questions! Just like I'm not allowed to ask *them* questions! Questions like, 'Why *do* I have to sit here all the time if silly school children don't shut the computer down?' or 'Can't I just go home for a bit?' or 'Can I at least go to the toilet?' *Oh no.*"

"Who's them?" said Fred.

"NO MORE QUESTIONS!!!"

"Actually, Mystery Man, can we just ask one more question?" said Ellie.

"NO!"

"Just one! About the Controller?"

"NO!"

Ellie shook her head and her mouth tightened a little, which, Fred knew, meant she was going to get tough.

"If you *don't* let us ask this question… we *won't* shut the computer down when we leave… again," she said.

The Mystery Man opened his mouth, possibly to shout "NO!" again – we'll never know because he then shut it. He opened it again and shut it again.

In fact, this happened four times before he said: "OK. One question."

Ellie held up the Controller. Fred held up his bracelet.

"What's happened to the Controller?"

The Mystery Man leant forward, peering at them.

"Hmm. Flashing."

"Yes."

"It's running out of power," he said matter-of-factly.

CHAPTER 32
Nerd

F red and Ellie looked at each other.

"OK. We thought it might be that. Where do we get a new battery?"

The Mystery Man leant back from the screen.

"Now *that*... is a second question."

Fred and Ellie looked at each other.

"Well," said Fred, "I'd say that, technically, it's a subsidiary second section of the first question."

The Mystery Man looked at him. "A *blubidury*

necond dection of the shmirst zecktion," he said, waving his arms about and doing a high, nasal, silly voice. Then: "Nerd," in his normal voice.

"I thought you were all about celebrating nerds?" said Ellie.

"That's *another* question."

"It was a rhetorical question."

"Nerd."

"LOOK!" Ellie shouted, suddenly standing up. Her chair screeched. "JUST TELL US WHERE TO GET A NEW BATTERY! AND, AS YOU MAY HAVE NOTICED, I HAVEN'T PHRASED THAT AS A QUESTION!!!"

The Mystery Man – and indeed Fred – looked a bit frightened. Ellie seemed to have grown more than just the seven centimetres added by the new look Fred had given her.

"OK, OK. Keep your – *new* – hair on."

Ellie sat down.

"So. Here's the thing. You *can't* get a new battery."

Ellie frowned. Fred frowned.

"What do you mean?" said Fred.

"It doesn't run on batteries."

"OK…" said Ellie. "How do we recharge it?"

"You don't."

Ellie frowned again. Fred frowned again.

"Sorry," said Ellie, "that sounded like you said… you don't?"

"Oh, sorry," said the Mystery Man. "Let me do that again." He moved his mic closer to his mouth. "YOU DON'T," he said again, so loudly now it distorted on the school computer's tiny speakers.

"So…" said Ellie, "that's it? It just runs out?"

"In my experience," said the Mystery Man, leaning back in his chair, "the Controller lasts just as long as it's *needed*."

Ellie frowned the hardest she'd frowned so far. Fred did as well, although his frowning ability wasn't quite as big as hers.

"What does *that* mean?" said Ellie.

The Mystery Man sighed.

"Now that really is a question I'm not going to answer…"

Ellie looked at Fred. Fred shrugged his shoulders. Ellie shook her head.

"All I will say is…" said the Mystery Man mysteriously,[21] *"many a mickle makes a muckle; a rolling stone gathers no moss;* and… *there are two sides to every story."*

He left a long pause after this, a half-smile playing on his lips. Ellie and Fred both narrowed their eyes.

"I think you're just saying anything that comes into your head," said Ellie, "to sound mysterious."

"Am I?" said the Mystery Man, raising an eyebrow

---

[21] I mean obviously mysteriously – he spoke mysteriously all the time – but he was adding extra mystery at this point. Like a special, added, extra shot of mystery.

to go with his half-smile.

"Yes," said Fred. They got up and turned away. The Mystery Man's face fell.

"OK, I might be. However…"

They turned back to the screen.

"Yes?"

"That new look you've got is very fetching, Ellie, but it'll be draining the power as we speak."

Ellie stared at him. Then she looked down at herself, at her different-from-usual clothes and different-from-usual body.

"Really?"

"Longer you keep that up, quicker it'll go down."

Ellie stared at him. Then she turned to Fred, handing him the Controller.

"Let's get home! Soon as poss!!"

Fred nodded and they both turned and ran out of the computer room.

"Hm," said the Mystery Man, smugly crossing his

arms. "I see *that* got through to them at least."

Then, the smug expression on his face faded. "Um… Fred?" he said. And then: "Ellie?" a bit louder. "You've… forgotten to shut the computer down again. Hello? Can you come back…? PLEASE? Oh no, the screensaver's up now. HELP!! HELP!! I'M BEHIND MR FAWCETT!! WELL, ACTUALLY, THE KOREAN KID HOLDING THE VIOLIN!! *HELP!!!!*"

CHAPTER 33
It's got a flashing light on it

"OK. So. Change me back to normal," said Ellie, looking at herself in the mirror in the playroom. The bracelet, on her right wrist, was flashing.

Fred poised his fingers on the Controller. "Right… do you want to say goodbye to it?"

"To what?"

"To… that look. That version of you."

Ellie turned to him. "Well. For now."

Fred's fingers remained poised. "What do you mean?"

"Well, obviously, I might want to look like this again… at some point."

"What point?" said Fred.

"I don't know. Whenever."

"Ellie. We can't keep using the Controller like this. The Mystery Man was clear. If we carry on using it and using it the power will run out."

Ellie narrowed her eyes at her brother. "So… what are we saving it for then?"

Fred looked shocked. "Me!"

Ellie laughed out loud. "You?"

"Yes! When I play in the final of the Bracket Wood and Surrounding Area Inter-school Winter Trophy! That the scout from Chelsea is coming to watch me play in!"

"When we got this, who decided that what you want is more important? It's *my* Controller!"

"In what way is it *your* Controller?"

"I'm the one who's better at video games! I'm the one who wanted a new controller! I'm the one who does *all the controlling*!"

Fred held up the Controller. "Apart from *now*. And any other time you need me to make you look like Cinderellie!"

Ellie stared at him. She took a deep breath. "Look. It's *both* of ours. Of course! But just change me back to normal for now – because we have to, because we know it's using up the power – and we'll work it all out later! OK?"

Fred thought about it. He wasn't sure. He felt they hadn't really talked about it properly. But he agreed that, as long as Ellie looked like Cinderellie, energy was draining out of the Controller. So he nodded, then very quickly ran his fingers over the buttons, and Ellie's hair, lips, height, skin colour, teeth and clothes all returned to normal.

She looked at herself in the mirror. "Great," she

said, although to Fred she didn't sound like she actually thought it was.

"Now what?" he said.

"Let's leave it here and make sure we don't use it until the day of the game." She took the bracelet off and put it on the floor of the playroom.

"OK," said Fred. "Good idea." He laid the Controller down next to it.

There was a pause as they looked at the Controller and the bracelet flashing together in time.

"What shall we do now?" said Fred.

Ellie thought for a moment. "Maths homework?"

Fred looked at her, in her glasses, and V-neck, and braces, and smiled. "Yes!" he said. And they both ran out of the playroom.

A few minutes later, Eric came into the playroom.

"Fred? Ellie?" he said. He looked around. *Kids,* he thought. *When you* don't *want to see them — like when you're watching Jamie Oliver tell you a fantastic bacon sandwich recipe on YouTube – they turn up (and steal the computer!). When you do want to see them – like now, when you're feeling a little lonely and dinner's over and the wife's stuck in front of the TV as usual – they're nowhere to be seen.*

Eric was feeling a tiny bit depressed. He had started to wonder recently if perhaps – what with Janine spending all day watching *Cash in the Attic* and Fred and Ellie spending all day playing video games if – well – if they weren't really a proper *family* any more. Because a family – well – they should do stuff together sometimes. Shouldn't they?

It's not as if there's anything I'm obsessed with that takes my focus away from the family, Eric thought. Then he thought about going back into the kitchen to see if there was any kind of special treat in the fridge, as he often did when he was a bit depressed. Perhaps the bar of bacon-flavoured chocolate that Janine had bought him for his birthday. Could there be any of that left? On no, he'd eaten it in one bite. Still, worth looking anyway – and then he saw, in the corner of his eye, something flashing on the playroom carpet.

With some grunting, he crouched down on the floor, picked up the bracelet and stared at it. *Quite a nice-looking one*, he thought. He held up his hand and put the bracelet on top of it. It sat there, like a headband for his fingers. It troubled Eric a little that it didn't slide easily down his hand. It suggested to him that, maybe, his fingers, and his hand in general, might be a little podgy. Using his other hand, he began pushing the bracelet down. It wasn't easy. He had to force it over his fingers. He squeezed them tightly together to get it to move downwards.

There was more grunting, and more forcing, but eventually he managed to get the bracelet past his hand and on to his wrist. Once there, however,

Eric wasn't sure why he'd done this. It hurt quite a lot. His wrist skin – that wasn't something he'd ever really thought about having before, *wrist skin* – bulged around it. He put his other hand on the bracelet again, with a view to taking it off.

But now it *really* wouldn't budge. It just hurt, and it hurt more to try and move it. So Eric did what he always did when he couldn't think of what to do.

"JANINE!!" he shouted. "*JA-NINE!!*"

"WHAT?" she shouted back.

"COME AND HELP ME!"

"WHAT HAVE YOU DONE?"

"I GOT STUCK!"

"STUCK WHERE?"

"NO, MY HAND GOT STUCK! ON A *BRACELET*!"

There was a short pause. Eric could hear, just, the sound of someone on the TV saying: "...so, if we just scrape the dust off her bottom, you can see – yes – it's actually a nineteenth-century piece of china..."

Then the door to the playroom opened. Janine stood there, arms folded.

"Right, so what you mean, Eric, is that a bracelet has got stuck on your hand. Which is *not* something that would stop you from coming into the living room."

"Sorry, Janine," said Eric.

"Let me have a look." She came over and held up his hand. "Hmm. It's quite pretty."

"Is it?"

"Yes. Might be worth a bit. Shall I call—"

"We didn't find it in the attic, Janine. We don't have an attic. *We live in a ground-floor flat.*"

"I know!" she said, with more than a hint of anguish. "Do you have to keep reminding me?!"

"*And* I don't think it's an antique. It's got a flashing light on it."

Janine sniffed. "Doesn't have to be an actual attic. Or an antique. The other week, in someone's shed, they found a digital watch that was worth—"

"Janine. It's hurting."

She tutted. "All right. Go and soap up your wrist in the sink and I'll see if I can pull it off."

Eric nodded and left. Janine watched him go. Then, in the corner of her eye, she noticed something else flashing.

She bent down and picked up the Controller.

"ERIC!" she shouted. "SHOULDN'T WE BE ABLE TO GET TV IN HERE? USING THE KIDS' VIDEO-GAME STUFF?"

"WHAT?"

"YOU KNOW. ALL THEIR VIDEO-GAME STUFF. THE Z-BOX. THE PLAY CENTRE. THE NINTENDO B. CAN'T YOU GET TV ON THEM AS WELL?"

She heard the tap go on. "I DUNNO!" he said.

Janine looked at the Controller. "Of course you don't," she muttered. She pointed the Controller at the TV screen. And pressed the emerald button.

While jiggling the control stick.

In the kitchen, Eric Stone found himself no longer washing his hands, but crouched on top of the sink. *Eh?* he thought. But not for very long because the next thing he knew something even stranger was happening.

CHAPTER 34
Two cowboys about to draw

Moments later, Eric was whirling round and round in the sink, with the tap water coming off him on all sides. It was like a beautiful fountain. If a beautiful fountain had had, at its centre, not a dolphin or a Greek god, but a whirling fat man.

"JANIIIIIIINEEEE!" he shouted, as he went round.

"OH NO!" she shouted back. "I'M NOT COMING TO YOU AGAIN! I'M FED UP WITH YOU SHOUTING

AT ME TO RESCUE YOU EVERY TIME YOU GET INTO THE TINIEST SITUATION! BESIDES, I'M TRYING TO MAKE THE TV WORK IN HERE!"

"BUT I'M NOT IN CONTROL OF MY OWN BODY!!" shouted Eric.

"Tell me about it…!" muttered Janine. Then, more loudly: "That's why I bought you the FATANX! Not that you ever wear it!"

And she pressed some more buttons. At which point, Eric spun out of the sink and across the room.

"*WOOOOAAAAHHHH! HEEEEEELP!!*" he screamed. But not loud enough to wake up Margaret Scratcher, who was sleeping on the floor next to the window. Where he was heading.

Splat! Eric's tummy landed with all its considerable wobbliness on top of Margaret Scratcher, who at that point looked more like Margaret Squished-er.

But she was OK. Eric knew this because, after the initial moment of squishing, he heard:

"*MEEEEEOOOOOWWWWW!!!*"

"WHAT'S WRONG WITH MARGARET?" shouted Janine.

"NOTHING, DARLING!" shouted Eric back, deciding, in this case, that it might be better to stay on top of the cat.

"*MEEOWOWWFglllhdt,*" said Margaret.

Everything for a moment was quiet. Eric breathed a sigh of relief. But then his stomach started moving. Without him doing anything.

This wasn't anything to do with the Controller, though, which Janine was shaking at this point to see if it contained any batteries. This was to do with Margaret. You know when a cat gets a mouse or a bird and they lie on their back and drum the mouse or bird frantically with their back legs? As a form of play-torture?

This was what Margaret decided to do to Eric's tummy.

At first – from Eric's point of view – it was kind of pleasant. It was like having a massage. Eric felt the waves of flesh vibrate and wondered, for a moment, if he should lie face down on the cat more often, as a way of perhaps reducing his waistline.

Then Margaret extended her claws.

"OW! OW! OW! OW!" said Eric, frantically jumping up, with Margaret attached to him.

"OH, WHAT IS GOING ON IN THERE? AND HOW DO YOU MAKE THE TV WORK WITH THIS THING?!" cried Janine, flicking the control stick on the Controller backwards and forwards. Eric – with Margaret stuck to his tummy like a very furry brooch – jumped up and down six or seven times in very quick succession. He jumped very high: in fact, he hit the ceiling every time, making quite a big dent in it. Margaret looked on, a bit confused as to the exact point of all this.

She leapt off Eric, landing and turning round to

look at him quizzically. Janine, in the playroom, just shook her head and randomly pressed as many buttons as she could.

Eric, his hair covered in plaster, adopted a martial arts pose, one knee bent forward and both hands out, karate-style. Margaret Scratcher, sensing trouble, arched her back and ruffled up her fur. It was like two cowboys poised to draw. Or two old aristocrats about to have a duel. Or a fat man and a cat facing each other, uncertain about how they ended up like this.

In the playroom, Janine pressed the gold button.

"*HAAAAY-YAAAA!*" said Eric, leaping up and kicking out and doing a hand-shuffle at the same time.

Margaret Scratcher said: "*Mew*," and started licking herself.

"*YA! YA! YA!*" said Eric, karate-chopping and high-kicking in a circle around the cat.

"Why are you making so much noise?" said Janine, finally coming through from the playroom, but with her head down and still fiddling with the Controller.

"*HIYA! OMI... YA!*" said Eric, whirling round towards her. "I DON'T KNOW! I DON'T KNOW WHY I'M SAYING THESE THINGS!"

"Oh, don't be stupid," she replied, but still without looking at him, and moving the control stick round in a circle and pressing repeatedly on the gold button.

"*HARRRRRRRR...*"

Eric sprang up into a horizontal flying position, fist forward, like Superman in flight. He actually hung there in the air like that for a couple of moments, the way cartoon figures do when they run off a cliff. And then, with a big "*...YAAAA!!!*", he flew forward towards her, karate-chopping the Controller out of her hands and sending it whirling across the room.

"ERIC!" said Janine, looking up at long last.

"SORRY!" said Eric, collapsing in a heap by her feet.

"DAD!" said Ellie, who had come back into the kitchen.

"MUM!" said Fred, who had also come back into the kitchen.

"WHAT ARE YOU DOING?" they said together. They didn't actually wait for an answer, though. Their eyes just followed the Controller as it wheeled in the air towards the window. Outside, they could see Derek White reversing out of his drive.

In a second, it became clear what was going to happen: the Controller was going to fly through the window, breaking its glass. But that wasn't, at the speed it was moving, going to be enough to stop it crashing down the Stones' front drive and ending up in the road at just the moment that Derek was going to pull out of *his* front drive, crushing it beneath the wheels of his large people carrier.

Everyone could see this was going to happen. In fact, Ellie even said, really fast: "Fred! It's going to fly through the window, and then crash down our front drive, and end up in the road at just the moment that Derek is going to pull out of *his* front drive, crushing it beneath the wheels of his large people carrier!!!!"

"I know, Ellie! What are we going to do? What are we going to—"

"Oh, it's hit the wall and dropped on the floor."

"Oh," said Fred. "Right."

CHAPTER 35
The Boxspital

"Oh no!" said Ellie, once she and Fred had moved the Controller to the safety of the playroom again. (Fred had stuck a Post-it note on the back, with the words _MUM/DAD! DO NOT TOUCH!_ underlined on it. While agreeing this was a good idea, Ellie pointed out that it never worked when they did that, as they often did, with special food meant only for them in the fridge.) "It's flashing faster now!"

"So's the bracelet!" said Fred. Which had finally come off Eric's wrist as a result of the whole family forming a kind of conga with Ellie at the front (then Fred, then Janine) and pulling at it. When it actually came off, with an enormous *pop*!, Eric had fallen over on his back and so had the conga, in opposite directions.

There had then been a small amount of uncertainty about what, overall, just happened. Eric had insisted that he had no idea why he had been whirling about in the sink or doing karate moves around the cat, but Janine had quickly lost interest in her husband's wittering and turned the TV on; and, soon after that, Eric had lost interest in trying to make her listen and said, "Have we got any snacks in?"

"Mum and Dad must've used up loads of power!" Fred continued.

"OK," said Ellie. "Yes."

"But it's the final next Saturday!"

"Yes. Well. We have to conserve power. No using the Controller again until the match. For *anything*."

A few months before all this happened, Margaret Scratcher had brought in a sparrow. When Eric had finally managed to get it away from the cat's clutches – which had involved him doing a lot of running around and stopping every so often to breathe extremely heavily, and a certain amount of Margaret looking like: *What? I've brought you a present. What's wrong with you people?* – the poor terrified bird had sustained a damaged wing and couldn't fly away. So Fred and Ellie had made it a kind of bed in a shoebox lined with red crêpe paper. Every day they fed the sparrow water, using a pipette. Amazingly, it worked: the sparrow lived to fly another day. Slightly wonkily.

They called this shoebox the Boxspital. And it was into the Boxspital that the Controller and bracelet went, lights flashing, it seemed, faster than ever. Ellie placed them in solemnly, as if they were sacred relics, or maybe like they were living things, the same as the sparrow.

For a while, they didn't know what to do. Since they were in the playroom anyway, Ellie suggested that they play a video game... just to pass the slowly unfolding time. But, try as they might, they couldn't find their old controllers. Both Fred's and Ellie's had been lost somewhere:[22] lost and forgotten all because of the Controller.

---

[22] Not, I should stress, anywhere near Eric's bottom – he had become much more careful about checking behind him before he sat down after that incident.

CHAPTER 36
Happy Christmas, Stones...

The following week was torture for Fred and Ellie. They couldn't play video games, but they still had to keep going into the playroom to check that the Controller hadn't stopped flashing.

Fred began measuring the flashing, thinking that would help in some way. He tried to time it using a stopwatch and, at another point, against his own heartbeat, which, he noticed, seemed to beat louder when he looked at the Controller.

Ellie ended up just staring out of her bedroom window. It was, she noticed, getting darker earlier and earlier, as the year began moving towards its end. That should, she thought, make the days go more quickly. Which, because she and Fred felt stuck at that particular moment, should have been a good thing. But it wasn't. It just made her feel like time was running out.

Eventually, after what seemed more like a year than a week, Saturday came.

"Let me just check again," said Fred as they arrived through the gates of Bracket Wood.[23] Ellie sighed. She was carrying the Boxspital.

"This is the last time. What if exposing it to light makes it lose power?"

"Oh. I hadn't thought of that."

---

[23] The school was open, even though it was a Saturday, because that's where the team was meeting to go to the final of the Bracket Wood and Surrounding Area Inter-school Winter Trophy.

Ellie made a *well, it's always me who has to do the thinking, isn't it?* face. But she opened up the Boxspital anyway. Inside, the lights were flickering fast.

"Do you think it'll be OK for the match later?" said Fred.

"It'll be fine," said Ellie, shutting the box. "We're nearly there now. Just as long as we don't use it up on anything—"

"Well, well, well."

Ellie and Fred looked up.

"*Really?*" said Ellie.

"Oh yes," said Isla. Her arms were folded and she had a smirk on her face that Ellie didn't like one bit. As if she knew something.

"I don't think a rematch is worth your while, Isla," said Ellie. "It was very embarrassing for you and your brother last time."

"Oh, was it?" said Isla.

"Yes, she's right, it was," said Morris, whose arms were also folded.

"Shut up," said Isla.

"Just saying," said Morris. "Specially the juggling part."

"I don't think it'll be that embarrassing for us this time, though, will it, Morris?"

Morris slowly shook his head. Fred and Ellie frowned. They weren't sure if he was doing it that slowly to increase the drama or just because he was generally slow in the head.

"Why not?" said Fred.

Isla's smirk grew wider, until it grew into a smile. But not a good smile. She nodded at Morris, as if ordering him to do something.

Which he did.

He unfolded his arms to reveal, on his right wrist, a black bracelet.

"Happy Christmas, Stones…" said Isla.

CHAPTER 37
Charged to the MAX

Fred and Ellie's mouths dropped open. Still with their mouths gaping – it was like two goldfish doing a dance routine – they turned their heads to look at Isla. Who unfolded her arms, to reveal, in her hands, the Controller.

Well. Not *the* Controller. Not Fred and Ellie's Controller. But one exactly like it.

"Where did you get *that*?!" said Ellie.

Isla's not-good smile grew wider still (it was

getting quite close to being a mad grin). "I knew something was going on with that controller you kept playing with. So I had a chat with some friends of yours… they are your friends, aren't they? Those two ultra-nerds in Years Two and Three. What are their names again, Morris?"

"Um… one of them – the girl – is called a colour. Red? And the boy's name is something… Welsh, I think. Red and Tom Jones?"

"We're sorry, we're sorry, we're sorry!!" said Scarlet and Stirling, appearing from round the corner (they may have been listening in).

"We didn't want to tell them, honest!" said Scarlet.

"No, we didn't! But she said Morris would stamp on our iPods!"

"You don't have iPods!" cried Fred.

"No! But we will in Year Five!"

"Morris will have left the school by then!" said Ellie.

There was a short pause.

"Oh," said Scarlet. "We didn't think of that."

"No," said Stirling. "Or the fact that by then, almost definitely, we won't be using iPods. I imagine we'll all be using the Zen FlashPlayer or the TDK ScreenCircus – both already in BETA development and— Ow!"

The "Ow!" was because Morris had flicked him on the eyebrow.

"And also…" said Scarlet, "you didn't want us to come with you to school when we offered to on FaceFace the other day."

"Yes," said Stirling. "Sometimes I'm not sure you like us at all!"

Scarlet, seeing her brother starting to sniff, began to sniff more.

Ellie and Fred looked at each other.

"Scarlet, Stirling," said Ellie. "Of course we *like* you! Don't cry – it's OK – we'll—"

"Well, it's a beautiful scene, I must say, but run along now… what do you call these two again, Stones?"

"iBabies!" the iBabies said, bursting into tears.

"Yes. Run along, iBabies!!"

And they did, as fast as they could go. Fred and Ellie looked on, unhappily. Nothing felt good about this.

"How sweet," said Isla, smirking. "Anyway, following the information garnered from your very close friends, we paid a visit to…" Here, she looked over Ellie and Fred's shoulders, towards something behind them, "…the computer room!!"

Fred and Ellie turned round. In the distance, in the main school building, they could see a window. On the inside of the room, facing the window, was a small screen. On the small screen, they could see a man waving with both arms.

"This morning in fact," said Isla. "And *he* was on

the screen…"

"The Mystery Man!" said Fred.

"Yes," said Isla. "Furious with you, he was. Something about shutting the computer down…?"

Fred and Ellie looked a bit ashamed. Isla made an *uh-oh!* face. Followed by a sarcastic, sticking-out-her-bottom-lip, *what a shame…* face.

"Anyway, we promised him – didn't we, Morris? – that *we* would shut the computer down… if he got us a Controller like yours."

Fred and Ellie looked at each other. Ellie frowned.

"This morning? How did it get here so quickly?"

"I dunno. How long did yours take to arrive?"

"But didn't you have to go home to get it?" said Fred.

"We *are* home Dumb-twin," said Isla. "Our dad's the head. We live here."

Ellie turned round again. The figure on the screen had stopped waving his arms and just looked sad.

"But you *didn't* shut the computer down…!" she said, turning back.

Isla made a *whatever* face and said: "Whatever. Anyway…" And here she raised her Controller up to face the twins. "Let's get on with it."

Ellie took a deep breath. "Listen, Isla… Fred's desperate to play in this game. And the school is desperate to win. We haven't won for ten years. And our Controller is running out of power… Can't we just be friends?"

Isla shook her head.

"OK, thought not. Well… can't we just *not* do this? Or do it next week? After the game?"

Isla's grin went through the roof. For a second, she looked like the Joker from *Batman*. If the Joker from *Batman* had been a somewhat precocious and annoying eleven-year-old girl.

"Sorry, I didn't hear most of what you said. The only words I heard in fact were 'our Controller is running out of power'. Which is interesting, from our point of view because, as you know, ours has just arrived. And is…" – she turned it round and Morris held up his bracelet: the blue light on both was pulsing slowly, perfectly in time, bright and clear – "…charged to the MAX!!!!"

Fred and Ellie exchanged glances. There was clearly no point in trying to reason with her.

"OK," said Ellie, opening the Boxspital with a heavy heart.

CHAPTER 38
EMWMWTAAPT Morris

A minute later, they lined up: Morris and Fred faced each other, with Isla behind Morris and Ellie behind Fred, Controllers at the ready.

"OK," said Ellie. "Press your buttons on the count of three. One… two…"

"Oh, poo to that!" said Isla, pressing the silver and gold buttons on her Controller together and flicking her control stick sharply forward.

Morris immediately jumped up. Fred expected

him to arc towards him with either feet or arms flying. But instead Morris swirled in the air, round and round; and as he swirled his body took on armour: a face mask with a metal grille, a bronze chest shield and what appeared to be a long black skirt.

The long black skirt made Fred laugh for a moment, but when Morris landed in front of him – and acquired, as the last bit of his outfit, a body-length bamboo stick – it didn't look funny any more… It looked…

"KENDO!!" Fred shouted to Ellie behind him. "She's made him a kendo warrior!"

"I know!"

"Can you kendo me up?!"

Ellie was frantically pressing the buttons on their Controller. "No! It hasn't got enough power. And I don't know how to do that. You'll have to—"

There wasn't time to tell him what to do as Morris was circling towards Fred with his bamboo stick[24]

---

[24] It's actually called a shinai.

whirling. Ellie instinctively put her fingers on the Controller and Fred immediately began dodging. Every time Morris brought the *shinai* down, Fred would leap out of the way just in time. *WHACK! WHOOSH! WHACK! WHOOSH!* went the air around them.

Isla frowned and twisted her control stick angrily. Morris turned to face Fred, raising his *shinai* high above his head. Ellie's thumbs moved fast. Fred ducked and kicked his leg out, bringing his opponent crashing down. Fred then jumped up with a big *"HIYAAAAAA!!!"*, intending to land hard on Morris's head, but Isla's fingers were quick too – and Fred's flight downwards was stopped, nastily, by Morris's black-gloved fist coming up and batting him away to the side.

THWACK!

Fred flew across the playground.

"OOF!" said Fred as he bounced off the school climbing frame.

Getting up, gingerly, Fred couldn't see Kendo Warrior Morris any more. *Perhaps they've given up*, he thought optimistically. *Or perhaps*, he thought – less optimistically – *the reason I can't see Kendo Warrior Morris is that coming at me instead is Enormous Muscly Wrestler-Man With Tattoos and a Ponytail Morris.*

"What's going on?!?!" he shouted back at

Ellie, who was running towards him, waving the Controller.

"She's activated a different character!" shouted Ellie. "Can she do that? Don't we have to start a new match?"

"Shut up and fight!!!"

Ellie saw the speed at which Enormous Muscly Wrestler-Man With Tattoos and a Ponytail Morris[25] was approaching, both fists forward. "Or maybe…" She pressed the amber button and jerked the control stick. Just in time, Fred leapt up – and EMWMWTAAPT[26] Morris powered past underneath him.

Now. One thing about being controlled by the Controller was that although it meant you could do all sorts of things that you couldn't do normally, in terms of jumping and fighting and even looking

---

[25] This is going to get complicated. I'll call him EMWMWTAAPT Morris from now on.

[26] See?

amazing, you were, at some level, still you. Which meant that Morris was, even as Kendo Warrior Morris or EMWMWTAAPT Morris, still Morris. And therefore quite stupid.

Which might be why he carried on running without realising what had happened for ten seconds after Fred had jumped up, and why he ended up crashing both fists forward into the climbing frame.

And getting his enormous arms stuck between four square rungs.

"*Aaaarrgggghhhh!!*" said Morris in a low, growly voice like you might expect an enormous muscly wrestler-man with tattoos and a ponytail to have. He tried to move his arms – you could see the veins bulging in his biceps – and said "*Aaaarrgggghhhh!!*" a few more times, but it was no good.

Enormous Muscly Wrestler-Man With Tattoos and a Ponytail Morris was stuck, in a primary-school playground climbing frame.

Ellie came over to Fred, who was crouching nearby, having landed safely from his big leap.

"Well done!" she said.

"Well done yourself!" he said. "Is there any power left in the Controller?"

Ellie looked at the light. "A small amount, I think. Come on – let's get to the game!"

"Hold on just one tiny minute," said a voice behind them: Isla's, of course. "Unlike you two... the boy in *our* twinship – although the more stupid one obviously – *isn't* worse at video games. In fact, he may even be as good at them as his sister."

"Thanks, Isla," growled Morris, his back still turned away from them in his stuck-in-the-climbing-frame position.

"No problem, Morris," said Isla. She leant through the rungs of the climbing frame and took the bracelet off Morris's wrist, while handing him her Controller. His hands, although his arms were stuck, could still move. He put his fingers on the buttons. Isla turned back to Ellie and Fred and slowly – really making a lot of the moment – slid the bracelet down her wrist.

"Oh, Isla… no…" said Ellie.

Isla looked at her coolly. "You're not the only one who enjoys changing how she looks, Ellie," she said. "Morris!"

Morris's hands moved, pressing the buttons. And Isla… changed.

CHAPTER 39
I AM KARABUKI!

In front of Ellie's and Fred's eyes, Isla morphed: she grew taller and her muscles expanded; her clothes changed. Suddenly she was wearing white combat boots that went up to her knees, a tight blue leotard and a sleeveless top covered in martial arts symbols; her hair became shorter, curled into buns and plaits; and her hands, bunched into fists and covered in long black gloves – WITH METAL STUDS ON THE KNUCKLES!!! – had become three times their normal size.

Fred stared at her, terrified. Then he looked to Ellie.

"Isla…" said Ellie again pleadingly. "Don't do this."

"I am not Isla any more," said Isla. "I am… KARABUKI!"

Ellie sighed. "OK, Karabuki. Don't do this."

In answer to this, Morris pressed their Controller's buttons and Karabuki whirled around, doing a series of lightning kicks so fast they propelled her like a high-speed helicopter towards Fred's terrified face.

"ELLIE! SHE'S NOT LISTENING!" shouted Fred.

"I KNOW!" said Ellie, whose hands had gone to her Controller – and only just in time. She made Fred, although still terrified, block Karabuki's kicks with a series of hyper-fast defensive counter-punches.

THWACK! BLOCK! *THWACK!* BLOCK! *THWACK!* BLOCK!

Karabuki's feet and Fred's hands together formed a blur.

After twenty seconds of this blur, they separated and faced each other about three metres apart.

"*AAAAAAAAHHHHHHAAAAA!!*" shouted Karabuki, jumping and curving in a circle towards Fred.

"*HAAAAAAAAAAAAHHHHHHHH!*" shouted Fred, jumping and curving in a circle towards her.

They met high in the air in the middle of the circle. Well, *met* isn't really the word. The better word would be… smashed. Or maybe collided-like-asteroids. Asteroids that had arms and legs moving like high-speed weapons. Like the spikes Ancient Romans used to put on chariot wheels.

The noise of them colliding is almost impossible

to describe in words. Maybe:

FWAAARTTBASHSMASHBLATCRUNCH
FWAPBLAMAAAHDUKDUKDUKSSSSSMMMMM
MMBAPSLAPSLAPHITPUNCHHITPUNCH
KICKHITPUNCH-OW**BANG!!!!!!!**

might kind of cover it. With a tiny under-noise, quite difficult to hear, of Morris's and Ellie's fingers tapping super fast on their respective Controllers.

For some time, the two fighters cancelled each other out. But Fred was more tired; and Ellie was more tired; and the Controller – their Controller – was more tired.

Eventually, a loose uppercut from Karabuki caught Fred under the chin and knocked him out of the air. He landed on his back on the asphalt: a particularly hard bit as well, a section of the playground which Bracket Wood hadn't had enough money to convert to the nice new soft type.

Ellie ran over to Fred, who was quiet. *Very* quiet.

"Fred!" she said. "Fred!"

From behind her, she heard the sound of two combat-booted feet landing gracefully on the ground.

"OK, Isla," said Ellie, without looking up.

"I AM KARABUKI!"

"Yeah, all right. You've won. Just leave us alone now."

Karabuki nodded and narrowed her eyes. "Maybe I will."

Ellie, ignoring her dramatics, turned with concern to Fred, whose eyes were closed.

So far, every time Fred had done all the things he was able to do via the power of the Controller, he hadn't seemed in any danger. Even if he'd jumped down from a roof or a tree, he seemed to be protected from harm by the magic of wearing the bracelet. But now... Ellie wasn't even sure he was *breathing*.

CHAPTER 40
Pure power

And then Ellie remembered something you could do to check if someone was or wasn't breathing.

She picked up the Controller and turned it round. On the other side was the shiny metal plate, still so shiny she could see herself in it, looking not like Cinderellie but just normal Ellie. But she didn't spend any time thinking about that. Instead, she placed it under Fred's mouth and nose, so similar to her own, and waited.

For a second, nothing happened.

For another second, still nothing happened.

Ellie felt a terrible fear in the pit of her stomach. She wished she'd never got the Controller – wished she'd never, in fact, played video games. She promised to someone – God, she supposed, although she didn't really believe in Him – that if only Fred would be fine then she would be happy never to play video games a—

Luckily, she didn't have to quite finish making that promise because, before she could say *–gain*, a tiny spot of condensation appeared on the shiny metal plate. It grew to a circle.

"Fred!" said Ellie. "Say something. Something to make me know you're OK!"

"She's powering up!" said Fred.

"What?"

Fred's eyes were now completely open. He was

completely awake and completely alive. And he was completely terrified.

"Isla!" he shouted.

"KARABUKI!"

"Karabuki! She's powering up! For an electric strike!"

Ellie didn't have to turn round to know instantly what he meant.

Morris was still stuck in the climbing frame, but his fingers were flying all over the Controller buttons. Karabuki Isla was kneeling on the ground, with both gloved fists pressed against the asphalt (actually right on the red line of the seven-a-side football pitch). A series of fizzing white-blue sparks surrounded those fists. The sparks were getting bigger and bigger, and the noise of them crackling louder and louder, building up into a huge surge of pure power.

"What are we going to do?!" said Fred.

"I don't know!" said Ellie.

"*HHHHHHHAAAAAAAAYYYYYYAAAAAAAAHH HHHH!!*" screamed Karabuki Isla, lifting her fists towards both Ellie and Fred.

As she did so, the sparks came with them, shooting as fast as – well, as fast as what they were – *lightning*, towards Fred and Ellie.

CHAPTER 41

...

When something like that happens – when, that is, a female superbully shoots lightning out of her fists at you – there isn't much time, to be honest, to think.

But despite that Ellie did, just before the lightning struck, notice, in the corner of her eye, a distant hand waving. It was the hand of the Mystery Man, up in the computer room, which, just at this moment, seemed a very long way away indeed.

He may just have been waving to say, as ever, *Oy! You still haven't shut me down!* But nonetheless, for Ellie, it called to mind something else. Something the Mystery Man had said when he wanted to sound extra mysterious:

There are two sides to every story.

This might have meant nothing – like the other things he'd said: *many a mickle makes a muckle* and *a rolling stone gathers no moss* – but for some reason, with the lightning approaching and his hand waving in the corner of her eye, the idea of everything having two sides *did* mean something to Ellie.

With her quick fingers, schooled for years on many controllers in the playroom, she flipped the Controller round. Flipped it round so that its shiny metal plate faced the lightning.

Then she and Fred closed their eyes and just hoped for the best…

CHAPTER 42
I've felt better

A number of school kids who were there reported what happened next as a kind of amazing natural phenomenon – like the Northern Lights, or a supernova, or a solar fireball. From a distance – from, say, Mr Fawcett's study, where in fact he was looking out, somewhat mystified by all the noise – it looked like an incredibly violent electrical storm had suddenly hit a small section of the playground. An electrical storm in which the lightning was heading two ways at once.

Hmm... he thought. *I must speak to Mr Palmer about that. He teaches all the science stuff.* And turned away from the window.

What he missed – perhaps luckily – was the sight of his own daughter, in the form of a female martial arts mercenary, being hit by that lightning as it came back at her, absorbing it for about ten seconds before screaming "*OHHHHHHHHH!!!*" and being flung backwards across the playground.

"Karabuki?" said Morris from his position within the climbing frame. He couldn't, of course, completely turn round, so didn't see that Karabuki had crashed, back first, into the school gates.

"*Urrgh*... I think... I'm Isla again..." he heard her say. And so it was. Luckily – for Isla – Karabuki's powerful body had taken most of the force of the impact. Unluckily for Isla, that meant that Karabuki had had enough. The video-game martial arts body just melted away, leaving the eleven-year-old girl Isla sprawled on the ground, not badly hurt, but badly shaken.

Ellie went over to Morris. He was crying.

"I'm stuck," he said, in between sobs. "My enormous muscly tattooed body is stuck! *Waaaa—* "

"No, you're not," she said. "No, it isn't."

She pulled him out of the climbing frame. His avatar too had melted away. Only he hadn't realised.

"Oh," he said.

Ellie looked at the Controller in his hands. It had lost all its lights and gone black. Not as in black, its normal colour. As in burnt.

"Maybe you should go and help Isla."

"Yes," said Morris. "Maybe I should." And he turned to go. Then he looked at Ellie. "Thanks, um, for helping me."

"That's OK," said Ellie. Morris nodded, slowly, like he had actually understood something, perhaps for the first time. And then went off towards where Isla was lying.

"Hey!" said a voice by Ellie's side. She turned. It was Fred.

"Hey yourself! Are you OK?"

"Well… I've felt better. But I'm sure I can still… play football!"

Ellie stared at him, trying to make out how true this was. Then she looked at the Controller and at his bracelet. The lights were still pulsing. Just.

"OK," she said uncertainly.

Part 3

HIGHEST
LEVEL

CHAPTER 43
A big, flat, cardboard shoe

"**F**red! Ellie!" shouted Janine Stone, rising from the TV as the credits played over a man counting some money. "Where are they?"

"I think… Fred said something about a football match today," said Eric. His voice was muffled and at first Janine couldn't tell where it was coming from. But then she realised.

"What are you doing in here, Eric?" she said, opening the door to the playroom.

"Oh, I don't know, J. I asked the kids to write a Christmas list, but they've not got round to it, so I thought I'd just have a look at the sort of stuff they like…"

Janine scanned the room.

"I think it's fairly obvious what sort of stuff they like."

Her eyes, though, suddenly alighted on something that *wasn't* a video game. She bent down to pick it up, holding on to Margaret Scratcher as she did so to stop the cat falling off her arm.

"Goodness," she said. "What's *this* doing in here? I thought it'd got thrown in the rubbish years ago."

"What is it?" said Eric.

"A big, flat, cardboard shoe. I bought it for Fred, to help him learn how to tie up his shoelaces…"

"Oh," said Eric. "It didn't really work, did it?"

Janine shook her head. "No," she said. "He still has to have someone else do it for him, doesn't he?"

"Yes," said Eric. "Mainly Ellie."

Janine nodded.

Then both of them looked at each other.

Guiltily.

"What time does the match start?" said Janine.

CHAPTER 44
The Bracket Wood and Surrounding Area Inter-school Winter Trophy

The Bracket Wood and Surrounding Area Inter-school Winter Trophy was an annoying name for a competition that was never won by Bracket Wood.[27]

If it had been called the Junior School Big Football Championship, or the Primary FA

---

[27] Even more annoyingly, its full name this year was actually the Fringe Benefits Bracket Wood and Surrounding Area Inter-school Winter Trophy. Because this year it was sponsored by a local hairdresser. You'll see who this is in a few pages.

Challenge Trophy, it wouldn't have been so bad. But the fact that Bracket Wood actually had their name in the competition – because it was the largest school in the area and because it was the only school in the area actually named after the area – made it all the more embarrassing that, as already stated, they had never won it. In fact, before this year, they had never even got into the final.

The competition, which had been going for ten years, had in fact been won every year by Oakcroft Boys, a much smaller school situated about half a mile away from Bracket Wood. Being much smaller, you might expect it not to be able to field such a good side. However, it was also a private school and, as such, had more money. And having more money meant it had better facilities – better pitches, better kit and, most importantly, better coaches. Their football coach, in fact, had always been Mike McTaggart, who it was rumoured had played for Liverpool reserves at the same time as Alan Hansen had been in the first team.

Oakcroft Boys – and Mike McTaggart – had, to be honest, become a bit smug about winning the Bracket Wood and Surrounding Area Inter-school Winter Trophy. Last year, they had beaten Geary Road seven-nil and, in Mike's speech afterwards, while he was holding the cup, although he had said, "Three cheers for the losers!", a number of people reported that he was laughing as he said it. And not in a good way.

It was pretty clear, anyway, that Oakcroft were particularly smug about beating Bracket Wood. For a start, they were late arriving: the match was meant to start at three and their team only arrived at 2.45. Fred and Ellie, who were also late – but not because they were smug: in their case it was because they'd been battling bullies transformed into video-game martial arts fighters – arrived at the same time. They had to walk past them all in the car park coming out of their plush-looking purple team bus.

"Oh, my giddy aunt!" they heard one of the Oakcroft boys say. "Bracket Wood must be pretty desperate!!"

"Yes," another one said. "I knew they were rubbish. But I didn't know they were actually fielding nerds!"

"Is that girl playing?"

"Wouldn't make any difference if she did! They look practically the same!"

"Ha ha ha!"

Fred ignored them. Especially the ha ha ha, which just sounded stupid. It wasn't even proper laughing; it was actually one of them saying ha, ha and then ha. But Ellie looked troubled.

Fred was just about to ask her what the matter was, or tell her not to worry about what those stupid Oakcroft numpties were saying, when he and Ellie turned into the ground where the match was to be played.

The final of the Fringe Benefits Bracket Wood and Surrounding Area Inter-school Winter Trophy was not held at the Bracket Wood football pitch. Because, as we know, that was just a bit of trampy old park. Instead, it was held at Broom Hill Playing Fields, which were the best playing fields in the area, and which just happened to be owned by... Oakcroft Boys School. Which made the final:

a) basically, a home game for Oakcroft

b) more humiliating for Bracket Wood, having to play the final with their name on it, that they'd never won nor even been in the final of, at their rival's playing fields

and

c) really irritating because the Oakcroft team arrived in a team bus, when they could easily have walked, seeing as the school itself was under half a mile away. Bracket Wood's team had walked. From Bracket Wood. Which was *two* miles away. They were supposed to come by school bus, but it was still in the garage. Since 2003.

In the middle of the playing fields was Oakcroft Boys School No.1 Pitch (they had five altogether). This one was actually surrounded by a stand, like a proper football ground.

When Fred and Ellie arrived at the ground, the

first thing they noticed was not how beautifully manicured the pitch was; nor how white and recently painted the lines were around it; nor even that it had *corner flags*, fluttering in the four corners like... well, like corner flags, and not like three twigs and an old jumper. It was the fact that the stands were full. There was a *crowd*.

Quite a lot of them were Oakcroft boys, of course, and their parents. You could tell this by how purple that end was. As we know, apart from Fred and Ellie,[28] very few children wore the uniform at Bracket Wood, so their team supporters, collectively, didn't look very green. By contrast, *everyone* wore the uniform at Oakcroft – which was a very posh purple (hence the bus – yes, Oakcroft had a matching *bus*). They also had a school badge – a lion, proudly prancing on top of three swords – which was on the blazer and also on the scarf. Loads of those scarves were presently raised above the heads of the Oakcroft

---

[28] And one boy called Gerald, who really was a weirdo.

section of the crowd, swinging from side to side, as the holders of the scarves sang their famous school song:

Oakcroft... Oakcroft...
We have never lost!
Oakcroft... Oakcroft...
To send your child here is quite a cost!

On the other side of the ground, not marked out by a single colour, and not singing their famous school song – because they didn't have one – was the Bracket Wood end. Fred and Ellie looked over. In among the crowd, they could make out: Mr Barrington; Mr Fawcett; Scarlet and Stirling; Isla and Morris; and, somewhere near the back row...

"Is that who I think it is?" said Fred, peering.

"I'm not sure..." said Ellie, peering too.

Then, very faintly, from the direction of their joint

peering, they heard a man's voice complaining: "It's a football match. They *should* have bacon rolls. Or at least hot dogs! Where are the hot dogs?"

"Oh, do shut up, Eric. You're making a fool of yourself."

CHAPTER 45
The next game

"**M**um!" shouted Fred and Ellie together, waving. "Dad!"

Janine looked over from the stands.

"Ooh, look, Eric!" she said.

"Have you seen a pie stall?"

"No! Look!"

Eric squinted into the distance. "Oh yes!" And he started waving back.

"It's amazing that they came," said Fred.

"Yes," said Ellie. But actually she didn't seem to be concentrating on what Fred was saying, or on her dad waving, or even on the number of other people her dad was knocking over accidentally as he waved.

"Oh, look!" Fred said, pointing excitedly.

"What?" said Ellie.

"Next to Dad. Just arriving. That's Sven Matthias!"

"Who?"

"The talent scout! From Chelsea! He came!"

Ellie looked over vaguely. A man in a smart black coat was shielding his head from Eric's big waving hands.

"OK," said Fred, drawing her attention back to him. "That makes it all the more important that we get this right. Where are you going to be controlling me from?"

"I guess… over there… with the school…" said Ellie.

"Great!" said Fred. But he could tell something was wrong with her. *Maybe she's just worried*, he thought, *because the Controller hasn't got much power left.*

Then he noticed that a table had been set up, behind one of the goals, and in the centre of that table stood the Fringe Benefits Bracket Wood and Surrounding Area Inter-school Winter Trophy. It was on a small plinth and so shiny you could see the reflection of the net in it. Just seeing it made Fred excited and, somehow, confident.

"We're going to win, Ellie," he said. "The trophy. It's going to be great!"

She looked at him. "Then what?"

"Pardon me?"

"Then what, Fred? So I control you today, like I controlled you in the last game. And we win because you play brilliantly. Then what? What happens at the next game, when we don't have a Controller any more?"

Fred frowned. "There isn't a next game. This is the last one of the season."

"Of course there's a next game! What, are you never

going to play football again after this? What about..."
and here she added something to her tone, something
very unusual for her: just a hint of *spite*, "playing for
Chelsea?!"

Fred's frown deepened. He looked down. It was the
first time Ellie had ever said anything that made him
feel hurt. "What's brought this on?" he said.

His sister turned away. As she did so, though, Fred
saw her glance quickly towards the Bracket Wood
supporters. He looked over.

Standing at the front of the crowd was Rashid. He
did a thumbs up at Fred. Fred did one back.

"Is this to do with... Rashid?" said Fred.

"No!" said Ellie, in a way that obviously actually
meant *yes*, even if you weren't her twin and knew – or
used to know – everything she was thinking.

"Is it because he's here and so you want me to
use the Controller to change how you look again?
Back to Cinderellie?"

"NO!!!" she said again, in exactly the same way as before (only louder).

"But if I do that," said Fred, "it'll probably use up all the power that's left!"

"Yes! That's why I'm NOT asking you to do it!"

"And also… that's why you're saying that it's pointless controlling me anyway, because of the next game…?"

She turned back to face him.

"Yes, Fred. The *next* game. And the one after that. To be really good at football, you have to practise and train and work. It takes time and energy and thought and dedication. This…" she pointed to the Controller "…is just a short cut. That you can't keep taking."

"I can't?" said Fred.

"No," said Ellie. "I can't control you into being brilliant at football for the rest of your life. And you can't make me look… look…" Ellie's face scrunched up and her voice caught in her throat: "...*like a Disney Princess* for the rest of my life."

"Well...I was thinking more Pixar than Disney actually..." replied Fred.

But Ellie wasn't listening. In fact, Fred realised, as he looked at her that, quietly, not wanting anyone else to see, she was crying.

Fred didn't know what to do. He hated to see his sister so upset. Her crying was making him want to cry.

He looked down. The Controller was still there, in her trembling hands.

Fred thought about everything that had happened in the last few months. They had got Margaret Scratcher off the roof; they'd cut Isla and Morris down to size; they'd got Fred into the school team; they'd made Ellie the belle of the ball at Rashid's party. But that had all been at the start. When he thought about the things that had happened more recently, all Fred could see was that they'd ended up having to fight the bullies again, more bruisingly the second time; they'd upset Scarlet and Stirling; and, for the first time ever, he and Ellie were fighting.

He finished thinking about all that and his face hardened a little.

"Ellie. Can you think *Street Fighter*...?" he said.

"Why?" she said tearfully.

"Just... do it..." he said.

She shrugged and nodded.

"Now press the main button and jerk the control stick sideways and upwards."

"What for?" she said. "It'll just use up the power..."

"Please," said Fred.

Ellie sighed deeply. And did what she was told.

Fred's arm, the one with the bracelet on it, retracted sharply and then came forward at incredible speed, in an upwards karate chop... expertly aimed not at Ellie, but at the Controller.

Together, brother and sister watched as it spun

from her hands and rose in the air, above the goals, above the crowd, out somewhere beyond sight, beyond the reaches possibly even of Broom Hill Playing Fields, even though they were the size, as we know, of at least five football pitches.

Fred looked across at Ellie, who was still staring up in the air. He was pleased with himself. He knew that he'd done the right thing. He knew she would think so too. They always thought the same way. Eventually, she turned to look at him.

"YOU STUPID IDIOT!! WHAT DID YOU DO *THAT* FOR?" she cried.

CHAPTER 46
There's only really one place

Twenty minutes later, the game was about to start. Mr Barrington's team talk was still ringing in the Bracket Wood XI's ears:

"So. Let's make sure that we back up any diagonal runs from midfields with quick one-twos and cross-field balls, although don't forget to stick to a diamond shape if they start counter-attacking down the flanks; meanwhile, switch between 4–5–1 and 4–4–2 with the inside players down the middle

– stick to our zonal marking at the back, play off the front men, knock it short, knock it long and, come final whistle, we'll have our hands on that trophy!!"

There had been a long pause.

"Sorry, Mr Barrington," said one of the boys eventually. "We didn't really understand what you just said."

Mr Barrington sighed. "OK. Just get the ball to Fred! And let him work his magic!"

At that, the rest of the team had turned to Fred and cheered. They even started chanting: "Fred! Fred! Fred!"

Fred had smiled, as best he could – he even thought about doing a little kind of royal wave, to imply how confident he was – but he didn't feel it.

And he felt it even less now, standing on the centre spot, about to kick off, looking at Oakcroft lined up on the other side. Everything about them seemed to be… better. Their kit looked better; their boots looked better; most importantly, their *bodies* looked better – they all looked about seventeen! The goalie looked like he had just started university! Where he'd been studying Goalkeeping and Extreme Tallness For Your Age.

Turning round, Fred could see the ten other players in his team gazing hopefully at him. He scanned the crowd, taking in the Bracket Wood supporters' section. They were all looking... *hopeful* as well.

He could see Mr Fawcett looking hopeful; he could see his mum and dad looking hopeful (although in his dad's case this may have partly been because he'd worked out that there would be enough time at half-time to pop out to a nearby sandwich shop); he could see Sven Matthias looking hopeful (about having found a new great young player); he could see Stirling and Scarlet looking hopeful (in between checking out other people's mobile phones and telling them how out of date they were); he could even see Isla and Morris, back to their normal selves, making not a bad job of *pretending* to look hopeful.

But he couldn't see Ellie. No matter how hard he searched.

One thing about Ellie Stone – one thing that probably helped her be so good at video games – was that she had *very* good eyesight when it came to tracking moving objects. When there was, say, a football, tennis ball or baseball moving about on a screen, she seemed to know instinctively where it was going to end up and, well before it got there, had already moved her screen football, tennis or baseball player to where he or she needed to be to hit that ball with his or her foot, racket or bat.

Which is a long-winded way of saying that, even though she'd been cross with her brother, she had watched the flight of the Controller carefully.

Carefully enough, in fact, to have quite a good sense of where it might have ended up.

However, you didn't actually have to have an eye that was really good at tracking the movement of objects in flight to know that Fred had managed to send it really high into the air; and that objects in flight that go really high in the air but can't actually fly – well, there's only really one place they tend to end up.

On the ground.

In pieces normally.

So Ellie was trudging across the outskirts of Broom Hill Playing Fields without much hope. Clearly, her and her brother's little adventure was over. A part of her didn't even know why she was bothering. Maybe they could put the Controller together again. Or maybe… maybe she just wanted to gather up the bits and give it a decent burial. Perhaps in the Boxspital.

But, even as she was thinking this, she did keep on looking up in order to work out exactly what path the Controller would have taken across the sky. And then, in the distance, she realised it wouldn't have landed on the ground at all. In fact, she thought she could see a glint – a tiny reflection of sunlight off its shiny silver plate – in the branches of… yes… that tree.

CHAPTER 47
What happened?

Meanwhile, back inside the ground, the game had just kicked off. For the moment, perhaps surprisingly, Bracket Wood were in possession. Barry Bennett[29] had the ball. "Fred!" shouted Mr Barrington. "Get up there! Into their box!"

Fred did as he was told.

---

[29] Some of you may have heard of this boy before in a book called *The Parent Agency*. He was in a coma for a while, and some weird stuff happened to him, but he's fine now and back at school. I don't think it was mentioned in the book he was in before, but anyway the school he went to was Bracket Wood. As it turns out.

"Right! Now, Barry! Kick it up to him!"

"Sorry?" said Barry.

"BARRY! CAN YOU NOT KNOCK IT??!!!" shouted Mr Barrington.

"Oh. Right," Barry said. He drew his foot back and kicked the ball forward, as hard as he could.

Fred was waiting in the Oakcroft box. He could see the ball coming. He looked round desperately at the crowd, in the hope that Ellie might somehow be there, with the Controller. But all he could see was his dad asking someone next to him if he could have some of his crisps.

Then he remembered: it was him – Fred – who had thrown the Controller away. It was him – Fred – who had realised that they – he and Ellie – couldn't live the rest of their lives relying on it. It was him – Fred – who had decided that he was going to play – AND WIN – this game, without help from some weird magic machine.

With that stirring thought, he drew himself up to his full height and jumped for the ball, knowing – just *knowing* – that it was going to come off his forehead cleanly and sharply into the Oakcroft goal.

Seconds later, his forehead made contact certainly sharply – but not, to be honest, especially cleanly – with the large muddy puddle behind the goal, having been sent there, face forward, by impacting quite hard with the three enormous Oakcroft defenders who had jumped in the air at the same time as him.

"*Ooofff!*" said Fred, who noticed that not only had he failed to achieve quite the same level of impressive sporting excellence as when Ellie and the Controller had been helping him, but also that, when he wasn't being controlled, stuff that looked like it should hurt, did. *Really* did.

He got up slowly. As he wiped the mud out of his eyes, he could see Oakcroft had taken the ball from their own penalty area right up the pitch and were advancing, very menacingly, on the Bracket Wood goal.

He could also see that quite a few of his own team – and Mr Barrington – were looking at him with expressions that clearly said: *What happened?*

Ellie, much like her brother waiting for the ball 450 metres away inside the ground, looked up with a yearning for the Controller. Only her yearning for the Controller to help her was also a yearning to *reach* the Controller, which was dangling on a tiny leafy offshoot of a big branch about halfway up the tree. It was stuck there, the tiny leafy offshoot holding it at the central point of the V formed by its two little branches.

She sighed. Ellie wasn't really a tomboy. Or at least, if she was, she was a modern tomboy, not an old-fashioned one. She was good at video games, not catapults and scrumping apples and *climbing trees*. But she had walked all this way and it had turned out the Controller wasn't actually in fifty pieces, so she thought she'd better give it a go.

She was about to raise herself on to the lowest branch of the tree when a voice said: "Can I give you a hand?"

She turned round to see Rashid smiling at her.

CHAPTER 48
Never even come near me with a football again

The policy of just giving the ball to Fred wasn't *quite* working. In that every time he'd got the ball so far, he'd been knocked off it and ended up in a muddy puddle. Not, at least, exactly the same muddy puddle. You couldn't fault Fred for his work rate: he was, as football people sometimes say, box to box – he was here, he was there, he was every jolly where – being knocked into muddy puddles.

He'd been knocked off the ball and into a muddy

puddle in the Oakcroft penalty area; he'd been knocked off the ball and into a muddy puddle at the centre circle; he'd been knocked off the ball and into a muddy puddle at all four corner flags; and – just now – he'd been knocked off the ball and *wished* he'd fallen into a muddy puddle in the Bracket Wood penalty area where, instead, he'd fallen into their own goalpost, banging his back quite hard. Which had left him too winded to get up and prevent the ball from going in.

The score presently was Oakcroft three, Bracket Wood nil.

As Fred finally got up, he saw most of his team walking sadly back to the centre circle. A number of them – and Mr Barrington, and a fair few supporters, he noticed this time – were looking at him with facial expressions that now said (as well as: *What happened?*): *You were really good in the last game and everyone thought you were our magic ingredient that meant we were going to win; but now, frankly, you're rubbish. We don't understand.*

They had got quite detailed, those facial expressions.

"What are you doing here?" Ellie asked Rashid. "Don't you want to watch the game?"

"A bit," said Rashid. "But I don't like real football that much."

"Real football?"

"Yes. I like *FIFA*. I basically like video-game

football more than I like real football. Because real football can get…"

"Boring!" said Ellie.

"Yes!" said Rashid. "But, when you play it on a video game, you can keep it interesting."

"That's what I think!" said Ellie.

"Oh good," said Rashid. "I'm glad. It's hard to find someone who agrees. So anyway… are you trying to reach that controller?"

Ellie wasn't sure what to say. But she guessed that lying hadn't helped the situation much so far. So she said yes. Then, feeling like she should explain, added: "It's in the tree because—"

"I saw. Fred karate-chopped it out of the football ground."

Ellie nodded.

"Amazing karate chop," said Rashid.

Ellie nodded again.

There was a short pause.

Then Rashid said: "Why did he do that?"

There was another short pause. Then, Ellie sighed and said: "Well. It's a magic Controller. I've been using it to control Fred. I work the Controller and when it's in sync with my brother, he's like my avatar on a video game and I can make him jump really high and fight really well and dig really deep and play football really well. But then it started losing power and we had a row about it and he kind of tricked me into controlling him to karate-chop it out of the ground."

There was a longer pause after this. Eventually, Rashid nodded and said: "OK. We'd better get it down then."

At half-time, with the score now at four-nil, the mood in the Bracket Wood changing room was not good. The players were all sitting on the benches, looking down at their boots. Prajit, who was really too small to be in goal – his nickname was the Cat, not because he was good at leaping and jumping, but because his dad was a vet and he sometimes smelt, therefore, of a mix of fur, cat wee and Whiskas – looked particularly depressed.

"So… shall we stick to the same plan for the second half, Mr Barrington?" said Barry Bennett after a bit.

Mr Barrington, who had been very quiet, and not actually doing what managers tend to do in this situation, which is shout very loudly at the team about how it's been a disgrace, shrugged his shoulders and just looked at Fred.

"What do you think, Fred?" he said. "Should we stick to the plan? Or should we change it?" Mr Barrington leant in towards him. "Should I, in fact, take you off?"

Fred held Mr Barrington's gaze. The teacher's eyes behind his glasses were huge and sad. Fred became aware that everyone else in the room was also looking at him.

As it happens, the last thing Fred had seen *before* Mr Barrington's huge and sad eyes was the even sadder sight, as he trudged off the pitch at half-time, of Sven Matthias heading for the exit. So he wanted to say, *Yes, please: take me off and never pick me again; never even come near me with a football again; never even SAY THE WORD "football" near me again*, but suddenly, as he thought about saying these things, he realised he might cry.

And so, because he didn't want to cry in front of the whole team, he didn't say anything.

And so, because Fred wasn't saying anything, Mr Barrington assumed he didn't want to come off and said, in a kindly voice: "OK. Go back on for the first five minutes of the second half and we'll see how it goes."

CHAPTER 49
Like this one?

"So... does it still work?" said Rashid.

Ellie brushed the last few leaves – and a small crumbling piece of bark – from her front before answering. It hadn't been an easy climb. But it had been quite exciting. Partly because it just was quite exciting, climbing a tree. But also because she'd been doing it with Rashid.

He had been pretty good at climbing, but even better at helping her from the ground – getting down on all fours to give her a step up in the first place, directing her to knots and footholds she couldn't see, and, once she'd rescued the Controller, holding out his arms for her to jump into on the way down.

"Come on!" he'd said. "I'll catch you!!"

"It'll hurt you!" she'd said.

"I think it'll be OK!"

So she had jumped, from the lowest branch. It *had* hurt him a bit, she thought – he did say "Ow!" – but that was maybe only because she was holding the Controller and one of its handles had hit him on the nose.

Then there had been a kind of embarrassing moment where she had just stayed in his arms for two seconds before they'd separated, standing about a metre apart and not saying anything. Then they'd caught each other's eye and laughed. And then Rashid had asked the question about how the Controller worked.[30]

---

[30] The one at the beginning of this chapter. In case you'd forgotten.

"I don't know," replied Ellie, looking at it doubtfully. It was covered in tree dust and the blue light was pulsing as weakly as she'd ever seen it. "I can't tell unless I sync it with the person wearing the bracelet."

"Bracelet?"

"Oh yeah. I forgot to tell you about that. It's a little black bracelet that comes with it and has a blue light on it, like… this one," she said, pointing to the Controller.

"Or… like this one?" said Rashid, producing from his pocket another bracelet.

CHAPTER 50
Paired

"Where did you get that?!" said Ellie, amazed.

"From Isla and Morris Fawcett," said Rashid.

"Oh…" said Ellie.

"Morris was wearing it. But Isla seemed to be a bit cross with him about it. 'Why are you still wearing that stupid thing! It just reminds me of how we got our butts kicked again!' she kept on saying to him. I didn't really know what she was talking about."

Ellie shook her head as if she didn't either. Rashid held out the bracelet to Ellie, who took it, and began examining it closely.

"Anyway, so Morris looked all ashamed," Rashid continued, "and took it off and chucked it away. But I quite liked the look of it. So I picked it up and put it in my pocket. Was that wrong?"

"No! No…" said Ellie. Who had noticed something: even though it wasn't the bracelet she and Fred had been using, the light on it *was* pulsing… more or less… in time with their Controller. Which might mean that…

"Rashid," she said. "Would you mind just holding the Controller a minute…?"

"I'd love to!" he said. She handed it to him. He cradled it in his palms, staring at it with awe. "It's amazing…"

"Yes, it is. Are you a gamer?"

"Yes!"

"What's your favourite game?"

"Oh, all the usual ones. But also, there's a really obscure one I love that my dad bought for me. It's Japanese: *Gravity Rush*. You fly about in it and have loads of adventures."

Ellie nodded. "Sounds great. Can you hold it up? The Controller…" she said.

"Hold it up?"

"Yes. Above your head."

"Like this?" he said, doing so.

"Yes!" Ellie put the bracelet on, and held up her arm, to touch its light to the lights on the Controller. Immediately, the blue lights started pulsing *exactly* in time with each other.

"Wow," said Rashid, looking up. "Does that mean… we're paired?"

"Yes," said Ellie. "Paired."

Rashid thought for a moment. "Can I make you do stuff now? Video-game stuff?"

"Um… yes. I suppose. But normally, I do all the controlling. I haven't really had a chance to feel what it would be like to… jump up buildings, or be amazing at karate, or anything. Fred got to do all that."

"Well, that's not fair," said Rashid, placing his palm flat down on all the Controller's jewelled buttons at once.

CHAPTER 51
Gravity Rush

"Woooaahh!" shouted Ellie, as she rose up into the air. "What are you doing?!"

"Making you fly. Like in *Gravity Rush!*"

"How did you know you were meant to think about a particular game when you do it?" She said each word a bit louder than the last as she was floating higher and higher each time she spoke.

"I guessed!" he shouted up at her.

"OK!" she shouted back. "But we can't do this for

long! The power's running out!"

"Sorry?" he said. "I can't hear you!"

"I said the power's running oowwwwwowwwww—"
She never quite got to the T (of 'out') because
Rashid flipped the control stick around, and she
began twirling, looping the loop, above the top of
the tree they had just climbed.

She looped the loop, and then she zigzagged,
and then she dived, and then she rose again, and
then she swerved to the left, and then to the right,
and then back around the tree, and then she just
hovered in the air for a while.

Looking down, she could see, quite
a long way away, Rashid smiling.
He waved at her. And Ellie, who
didn't often do this, let go of all
her cares. She stuck her arms
out and – as Rashid threw the
control stick forward – she flew.

She flew.

A bit later, after he'd expertly brought Ellie down to the ground, and they'd begun walking back towards the football pitch, Rashid, who was still holding the Controller, said: "It's incredible. Does it do anything else?"

"Um… well," replied Ellie. "You can also use it to change the way someone looks… make them have different hair and features and stuff. You can make the person wearing the bracelet look…" and here she glanced down at her wrist, remembering that at this moment, *she* was the person wearing the bracelet "…however you want them to look."

Rashid looked at her. Suddenly, he stopped walking, and stared at the device, frowning. Ellie stopped too, and braced herself. She was pretty sure she knew what he was going to do next.

But he just handed the Controller back to her, and said: "Why would anyone want to do that?"

And ran off towards the football ground.

Ellie paused for a second, then looked down at the Controller. She was holding it upside down; on the shiny plate on the back, she could see a reflection of her own face. Her own face, that is, with its glasses and its braces and its pigtails: and a very big smile.

Then she ran after Rashid.

CHAPTER 52
When it comes to
the crunch

S ven Matthias had seen enough. He was a busy man and he didn't have time to hang around. He was, however, a little confused. He had very good instincts for talent. And he knew those instincts had been set alight by seeing this Bracket Wood boy play in the semi-final.

So now, standing outside the little ground in the middle of the posh school sports field, he was disappointed – and somewhat bewildered – by how bad the kid seemed to be in *this* game, the final. *Maybe*, he thought sadly to himself, *this one just can't do it when it comes to the crunch, in the biggest games.* Better to know that now than, say, in ten years' time at the Champions League Final.

He took out his phone.

"Hi, John?" he said. "It's Sven. I'm leaving. Yes, at half-time. Can you bring the car round to—"

"Excuse me, Mr Matthias?" said a small voice. He looked down. A young girl with braces and glasses and pigtails stood there, next to an Asian boy of about the same age.

Sven moved the phone away from his ear.

"Yes?" he said.

"Can I just hold you up for a second?" she said.

CHAPTER 53
Single bow

The referee blew his whistle to start the second half. Oakcroft's players passed the ball around between themselves. It looked like they were toying with the game now. As if at any moment they could just take the ball up into Bracket Wood's half and score.

Fred watched them from his own half disconsolately. He felt cold and tired. He had given up. Then he heard, distantly: *Fred! Fred! Fred!*

It's someone chanting, like the team did before the game, he thought. Sarcastically now, of course. Probably a joke. But still it continued.

Fred! Fred! Fred!

Reluctantly, he looked in the direction of the chant. It was coming from somewhere towards the front of the Bracket Wood supporters' section.

What he saw surprised him.

His mum and his dad were chanting it. And pointing. Rashid was chanting it. And pointing.

Then Fred realised that they weren't chanting. They were just trying to attract his attention. He realised this because of who they were pointing at.

Ellie. Who was also shouting his name. And holding up the Controller.

"Fred!" she was shouting. "Fred! I found it!" She twisted the control stick and pressed the buttons as she shouted. Rashid and Eric and Janine were all giving a big thumbs up.

Fred felt the surge of power from the Controller rush through him. He just had time to return the thumbs up before speeding towards the ball.

The Oakcroft players were still casually knocking it about. One of them saw Fred coming and laughed. Others got ready to deposit him, as usual, in the mud.

But Fred took the ball away from them effortlessly. He flicked it off the boot of the player in possession and then dodged left, then right, evading every challenge. Then he ran on goal. The enormous keeper came out, smirking. But soon stopped smirking as Fred shot early, chipping the ball over his head – and over his too-late outstretched hands – into the net.

The Bracket Wood fans, who had gone very quiet – and stayed very quiet for a long time – burst into cheers. Fred hardly heard them because he was doing that thing that footballers sometimes do of picking the ball out of the opposing net and rushing back to the centre circle in order to get on with the game. He scored three more goals, each better than the last. He scored one with his right foot, one with his left, one with his head and one with an incredible overhead kick.

WHOOSH

He did volleys and back-heels and 360-degree turns and drag-backs and step-overs and zigzags and a new move that there wasn't a name for, but which involved flicking the ball with the back of his heel on to the top of his head, then bouncing it on his head over and over again while running down the wing.

There was one weird moment when his shoelaces came undone. Fred thought this was strange as his shoelaces hadn't come undone before when he was being controlled by the Controller. So he ran over to Ellie to tie them up.

But, as his sister went to bend down, Janine suddenly stood in front of her and said: "Excuse me. I've got this." And tied his laces in a very tight single bow that didn't come undone for the rest of the game, but also wasn't too bulky. Which allowed Fred to continue with his incredible performance.

By the end, the Bracket Wood supporters

were all chanting, "Fred! Fred! Fred!" completely unsarcastically.

But even all Fred's best efforts only meant that the score was four-all. A draw. So the game went to penalties. Which was worrying, as obviously Fred wasn't the only one who was going to take them.

But what Fred's performance had also done was *inspire* his team-mates. They had watched him raise his game, and they'd raised theirs too, passing and moving and supporting each other, and doing their very best as a team. Fred was the spearhead, but the rest of the team were the spear.

So, when it came to it, the players – Barry, Lukas, Taj and Jake[31] – who took the first four penalties put their heads down, hit the ball as hard as they could and scored!

Unfortunately for them, so did the first four Oakcroft players.

But the wind had changed in Bracket Wood's

---

[31] Barry's friends also went to Bracket Wood.

favour. The pressure was all on the Oakcroft player as he came up to take the fifth penalty.

He was actually the one who had laughed at Fred as he'd come towards them. He was also the one who had said, "Oh, my giddy aunt! Bracket Wood must be pretty desperate!!" But it was he who looked pretty desperate now.

He ran tentatively towards the ball and kicked. It was on target. It was heading to the top corner. But then Prajit proved that his nickname *wasn't* just because he sometimes smelt of fur, cat wee and Whiskas – no! He leapt like a tiger across the face of the goal, stretching out his hand to knock the ball over the bar!

Which made the penalty shoot-out score so far:

OAKCROFT 4

BRACKET WOOD 4

with one penalty to go.

The referee put the ball down on the spot and Fred came forward.

CHAPTER 54
WATCH OUT!

Fred faced the Oakcroft keeper. Who was looking VERY tall. Fred remembered reading that, as a child, Lionel Messi had been given growth-hormone treatment by Barcelona because he was too small and wondered, in this moment, if the Oakcroft keeper should not have been given whatever the reverse treatment was.

A hush descended on the ground. A shard of light from the late afternoon sun glinted off one of the handles of the Fringe Benefits Bracket Wood and Surrounding Area Inter-school Winter Trophy, still there behind the goal.

Fred suddenly felt nervous. Knowing the Controller was back in action had really bucked him up at the top of the second half, but now, faced with this monster in goal – and everyone in the school looking at him, relying on him to do well – the butterflies grew in his stomach to the point where it felt like there was a whole hothouse full of them in there.

His eyes searched the Bracket Wood supporters' end. Where was she? Had she gone again?

But no: there she was. Ellie. Holding the Controller above her head, her fingers poised on the control stick and buttons, her eyes burning.

What are you going to make me do? he mouthed.

And she mouthed back: *The cleverest, trickiest, most awe-inspiring move ever!!!*

Fred smiled; he felt the butterflies in his stomach all flutter down and settle. He turned back to the giant keeper, who had put both his arms out to make himself even bigger, and who appeared now to be... snarling. He was a snarling, arms-out giant. Fred turned round and walked away from the ball.

Bracket Wood supporters in the crowd – and his team-mates, standing with their arms linked on the centre line – whispered to each other.

"Oh my God! He's bottled it!"

"Please don't go back to the changing room, Fred!"

"OH NO!"

Whereas Oakcroft supporters in the crowd – and their team, also standing on another section of the centre line with their arms linked – said loudly: "Ha ha! He's bottled it!"

"He's walking back to the changing room, the

big *nerd*!"

"OH YES!!"

The referee looked a bit confused. He was just about to blow the whistle, awarding the game to Oakcroft,[32] when Fred stopped walking, bent his legs and… threw his body backwards!

"BACKFLIP!!!" shouted the Bracket Wood supporters.

[32] I know this is technically not quite right, as at this point the score is four-all. But the referee, who is not a big character in this story so I have decided not to give him a name, had decided in that moment that refusing to take a penalty because you were too nervous was such a big failure that it was basically equivalent to losing a goal. At least that was his thinking. He told me afterwards.

Yes! It was! He backflipped not once, not twice, but three times, throwing the Oakcroft keeper, who had been smirking in derision at Fred's retreating back, into confusion. He looked away, towards his team-mates, which was a mistake, as that was the point during Fred's last backflip that he twirled in the air to face forward, brought his right foot back and then swung it hard towards the ball, landing and connecting at the same time.

"OY!!!"

"DON'T LOOK AT US, LOOK AT THE BALL!"

"WATCH OUT!!"

These were just some of the things shouted at the keeper by the Oakcroft contingent. But, even if he hadn't been looking the wrong way, the keeper probably wouldn't have got to the ball in time because the momentum of three backflips coming through Fred's right foot sent it hard, fast and direct into the back of the net.

CHAPTER 55
110 per cent

The whole of the Bracket Wood end erupted. Fred could see them jumping up and down like they were all on individual trampolines. It was the last thing he saw for a little while, however, because all his team-mates had rushed over as soon as the ball had gone in and bombed on top of him in a happy pile.

Fred! Fred! Fred! went the chant.

Fred! Fred! Fred!

Once they'd finished piling on top of him, they lifted Fred on to their shoulders and carried him towards the trophy table. The crowd came out of the little stand and formed two walls of people round the path to the table, chanting and clapping as he went past. Then he noticed – it was easier being at shoulder height to see faces – that one of the people clapping and chanting was…

"Mr Matthias!" he said.

"Hello, Fred. Great game. I'm going to be in touch."

Fred thought his soul was going to burst with joy. "But… I thought you left at half-time."

Sven smiled. "I was going to, but I didn't. Thank your sister—"

"Fred!!!" shouted Prajit from underneath him. "Please can I put you down now?!"

"Oh, sorry, Prajit, yes," said Fred.

Prajit bent – well, sort of fell – down, and Fred

dropped off his shoulders and carried on towards the trophy table. Standing behind it was Mr Bodzharov.[33] Of Fringe Benefits.

"Well done, Fred. That is your name, isn't it?" said Mr Bodzharov, shaking his hand.

Fred nodded.

"I thought so. You played very well. Some of your moves reminded me of the great Hristo Stoichkov. Of course you won't have heard of him."

"Played for Bulgaria between 1986 and 1999."

Mr Bodzharov looked amazed.

"He's in my *FIFA* all-time XI," said Fred.

Mr Bodzharov smiled, looking very pleased. Then he suddenly produced a microphone and turned to the crowd.

"Fringe Benefits are very proud to have sponsored the Fringe Benefits Bracket Wood and Surrounding Area Inter-school Winter Trophy. And, just as both teams gave 110 per cent today, we at Fringe Benefits

---

[33] Yes, the very same. Told you you'd find out in a few pages.

give 20 per cent off all haircuts – not including blow-dry – before 5pm, Monday to Friday. Cash payments only."

This was greeted by silence, apart from a couple of people whispering, *Does that make sense?*

"Anyway," he continued, picking up the trophy, "well done, Bracket Wood! This year's winners of the—"

"Don't say Fringe Benefits again!" shouted a distant voice from the crowd.

"—Fringe Benefits Bracket Wood and Surrounding Area Inter-school Winter Trophy!!"

Everyone clapped and cheered as Mr Bodzharov held up the trophy. They were expecting him to hand it to Fred, so that he could turn round and hold it up to the crowd, like footballers do when they win big cups. But instead – perhaps wanting to draw out the moment for a bit longer (after all, the sponsorship, it was rumoured, had cost Fringe Benefits nearly

£100) – he held the microphone out to Fred and said: "Would you like to say a few words…?"

Fred was surprised. But then looking round at the crowd – at all the Bracket Wood pupils, and Mr Barrington, and Mr Fawcett, and his mum and dad, and Sven Matthias, and Rashid Khan, Stirling and Scarlet and even Isla and Morris, all clapping and smiling – and at Ellie, in the middle of this crowd, Fred decided he should indeed say a few words.

CHAPTER 56
A gentle little push

"I don't know if you do this when you win a football trophy," Fred began. He then stopped for a second, as he'd never heard his voice through a microphone before and it sounded really strange. "Is that what my voice sounds like?"

Everyone nodded.

"Weird. Anyway, I've seen it done when people win an award – like an Oscar and stuff – and they *thank* people. Other people, I mean. The people who've helped them get where they are. Sometimes they thank God, don't they? Anyway, I'd like to do that…"

"Thank God?" said Eric.

"No."

"Thank God," said Eric. "Thought he'd gone mad."

"I'd like to thank… well, you two. To start with. My mum and dad. Eric and Janine Stone…"

There was a ripple of applause. Eric and Janine beamed.

"When people get an award, they often thank their mum and dad, don't they? And they say, 'for always believing in me – when the rest of the world didn't' or something. I don't really know how much my mum and dad believe in me. I think what my dad believes in, mainly, is bacon sandwiches and what my mum believes in, mainly, is *Cash in the Attic*…"

Eric and Janine stopped beaming.

"…but it doesn't matter. Because that's who they are and I love them, and they've come here now to support me and that's great!"

Everyone clapped. Eric and Janine went back to beaming.

"I'd also like to thank Mr Barrington."

Mr Barrington beamed.

"Even though he didn't believe in me much either… He only put me in the team for the first time in the last game. And he nearly took me off at half-time in this one."

Mr Barrington stopped beaming.

"But still, another manager wouldn't have put me in the team at all. And he's really nice."

Everyone clapped. Mr Barrington went back to beaming.

"I'd also like to thank – for helping me in lots of ways, especially techno ones – from Years Two and Three, Scarlet and Stirling!"

Everyone clapped.

"You can call us iBabies!" shouted Scarlet.

"Yes!" shouted Stirling. "We like it. Although I was

going to suggest iBabies OX 10.4 as, like, an upgrade!"

Luckily, the applause covered up whatever else Stirling went on to say. Meanwhile, Fred realised his speech was starting to go on a bit – and was also possibly not the speech he thought he was going to make – so he decided to hurry it up.

"And I'd also like to thank my team-mates, and Oakcroft, and even Isla and Morris Fawcett, despite them being the school bullies…"

"Are you?" said Mr Fawcett, looking at them sharply.

"…who have tried to beat me up lots of times, including just now, when I was on my way here…"

"Did you?" said Mr Fawcett, his sharpness becoming even sharper.

"…but if it wasn't for them I wouldn't even have got good at football because it was them who knocked the computer over in the first place and – well, it's a long story, but I think I'm going to tell it. Because it brings me to the person I most want to thank…"

He looked up and found her in the crowd.

"My sister, Ellie," he said. "And here's why."

He was about to launch into it – to tell the whole thing, to everybody – when he saw that she was mouthing: *NO*.

Why not? he mouthed back. *I want to. I want everyone to know that you're the one. That you're the genius basically. That I didn't do it all by myself.*

Ellie smiled. Her eyes were moist. *No. YOU did. You DID do it all by yourself*, she mouthed.

What do you mean?

She held up the Controller. Fred squinted at it.

It's run out of power, she mouthed. *Or rather it RAN out of power. Before I even came back in the ground. Before the start of the second half.*

Huh? So why did you hold it up at me? Why did you operate it? I saw your fingers on it, all the time.

I was pretending. I could tell you were looking. So I pretended it was working.

Fred frowned.

Why?

Ellie smiled more. *Because I know you. Because you're my twin. I knew that you were brilliant. I knew you could be an amazing player. You just had to BELIEVE that something was making you brilliant.*

Fred shook his head. *I did all that – four goals, all those amazing tricks, the backflip penalty! – by myself?*

Yes, mouthed Ellie. *Because all you really needed to believe in… was yourself.*

There was a long pause. And then Mr Bodzharov said: "Are you all right, Fred? You seem to be opening and closing your mouth a lot with no words coming out. Are you having some sort of fit?"

Fred shook himself out of the trance all that mouthing had put him in. "No! I'm fine." He turned back to the crowd. "That's it really. Ellie. I'd like to thank Ellie. Just for being such a brilliant sister. Come up here, please!"

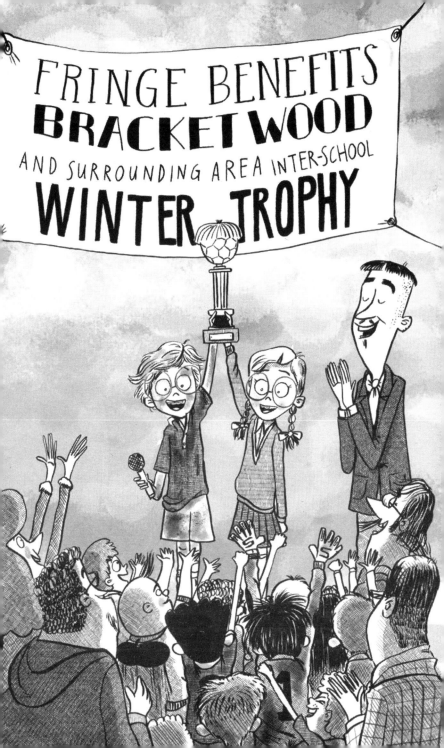

Ellie looked like she didn't really want to. She wasn't entirely sure about going up there and lifting the trophy with him and sharing the moment. But then Rashid, who was standing next to her, gave her a gentle little push.

Sometimes that's all we need.

Part 4

BONUS

WHAT HAPPENED
TO EVERYBODY AFTERWARDS – LIKE
AT THE END OF A FILM, YOU KNOW, OR THE
CUT SCENES AFTER THE CREDITS ON A GAME...

Sven Matthias is on the lookout for new players. So watch out for him if you're playing, even in the park, or at school!

Derek White and his family have moved to Lapland. And taken all their Christmas lights, despite the fact that there is nowhere to plug them in in an igloo.

Mr Barrington has decided to try contact lenses.

Mr Fawcett came to understand that Isla and Morris were perhaps not the ideal Bracket Wood pupils after all. They haven't won a certificate for good behaviour for a while. Having said that, they haven't bullied anyone for a while either. They may have learnt their lesson.

Prajit no longer sometimes smells of fur, cat wee and Whiskas.

Because his dad took early retirement.

Stirling and Scarlet are still not quite in Year Five, so still not quite able to deploy their techno-knowledge as they would like to. However, their mum has decided that their stepdad will no longer cut their hair.

Mr Bodzharov is OK with this as, since Fringe Benefits' sponsorship of the Fringe Benefits Bracket Wood and Surrounding Area Inter-school Winter Trophy, business is booming. He has recently opened a new sister shop to Fringe Benefits called Hair Today, Gone Today Also.

Eric has given up bacon sandwiches. And is on a new diet. It's called the Full English Breakfast diet. You eat full English breakfasts for every meal. But with NO toast. And sweeteners instead of sugar in your tea.

And Janine no longer watches TV all day. She now records daytime TV and watches it at night.[34]

---

[34] In bed. She has to turn up the volume quite loud to hear it over Eric's snoring.

Margaret Scratcher is exactly the same.

Fred went on to have a trial for Chelsea. In which he played really well. He's now in the junior squad!

And Ellie, meanwhile, is designing her own computer games. Rashid is helping her...

That's it, isn't it? Everybody important.

So anyway – thanks for reading it and—

Sorry, can you hear something...?

Someone saying... sounds like... "Shut me down!

You forgot to shut me down! I'm still on the screen!!!"

Strange. I can still hear it.

"Look, if you shut me down, I'll get you ANOTHER

Controller! I will! Made of SOLID GOLD!! THAT CAN

MAKE THE PERSON YOU'RE CONTROLLING...

INVISIBLE! AND FLY! AND RUN AT 20,000

MILES PER HOUR! And this one... this one will last

FOREVER!"

Hmmm. Might just be the wind.

Oh, OK. Just one more bit.

CHAPTER 57
Bonus Easter egg. On Christmas Day

Janine and Eric and Margaret Scratcher watched as Fred and Ellie tore open their main present. Their excited faces were lit gold, green and red by the fairy lights hanging off their little tree. In the background, on the radio, Slade were singing about Grandmas coming to stay and room to spare inside.

"Oh! It's a new video game!" said Fred, holding up a box.

"*Four* video games," said Eric. "It's sort of a box set.

All your favourites: *FIFA*, *Street Fighter*, *Super Mario* and *Minecraft*."

"The newest, most up-to-date versions of those games. Of course!" said Janine.

"And look, Fred!" said Ellie. "A new controller to go with it!"

"Yes..." said Eric. "I still feel bad about sitting on that one you liked. And then the new one you had for a while – I don't know where that went. I hope this one's all right."

Ellie held it up. It was a normal controller, black with green, red and blue buttons. "It's lovely," she said. "Thanks, Dad."

"So I suppose..." said Eric, "you want to go straight into the playroom and try it out. Don't worry. You can if you like."

"It's Christmas Day, isn't it?" said Janine. "You can do whatever you like."

Fred nodded and smiled. But then said: "Dad...

I really like the video-game present. But look outside! It's snowing!"

Eric turned his gaze to the window. He felt goose pimples rise on his flesh at the sight of it, at the idea that it could, after all, still snow on Christmas Day.

"Oh yes!"

"Can we go out and play in the snow, Dad?" said Ellie. "We'll do the video game later!"

"But you're in your pyjamas."

"It'll be more fun like that!" said Fred.

Eric and Janine exchanged glances.

"Of course!" they said together. "Go on!"

Fred and Ellie got up and began to run out of the door of the living room. Meanwhile, Eric and Janine exchanged one more glance.

"Fred. Ellie," said Eric, stopping them as they reached the door. "Is it all right... if we come and play?"

Fred frowned. Ellie frowned. Then *they* exchanged glances.

"But you've got your pyjamas on too...?" said Fred.

Janine got up, putting out her hand to help Eric heave himself off the sofa.

"Like you said, it'll be more fun like that..." she said.

And out of the door the whole family flew, cheering and shouting as they went.

If you'd been in the Stones' living room that Christmas Day, you'd have seen them through the window, building snowmen, making snow angels and throwing snowballs at each other for ages and ages. And, if you'd stayed long enough, you'd have seen one particular snowball hit the window quite hard. As it did so, a light, a blue light, on the controller that Ellie had left lying on the couch, pulsed. On and off.

But it had stopped by the time they came back inside; and the snowball on the window had turned to water.

Acknowledgments

Many thanks, for all their help in lots of different ways to do with the creation of this book, must go to everyone at HarperCollins Children's Books – particularly Nick Lake, Samantha Swinnerton, Kate Clarke, Elorine Grant, Manda Scott, Geraldine Stroud, Nicola Carthy and Ann-Janine Murtagh. Thanks must also go to: my illustrator, Jim Field, for co-creating these worlds; my children, Ezra and Dolly, who provided, as ever, very useful advice about being children, and also, in this case, about video games; my agent Georgia Garrett, who offered some late, but not too late, passionate suggestions; and Morwenna Banks, who calmly put up with the stuff she always has to put up with when I'm writing a book, even one this fun.

A new body-swap blockbuster from Baddiel!

Illustrated by Steven Lenton

Bracket Wood is about to be visited by school inspectors. And there's one BIG PROBLEM:

Ryan Ward

The prankster prince. The scourge of teachers. The naughtiest kid in school.

But when Ryan finally goes *too far* the head teacher, Mr Carter, arrives. A man so *strict* even the teachers are afraid of him. So imagine his surprise when they swap bodies. Now Ryan is in charge. Which is AWESOME.

Until… it isn't. Soon Bracket Wood School goes off the rails completely – and only its *worst* ever pupil can fix it.

Read an extract from David Baddiel's first hilarious book,
THE PARENT AGENCY.

We join the story as Barry's just had a HUGE argument
with his parents...

Barry lay in his bed, fuming. He'd gone straight to his room, without cleaning his teeth or anything, and slammed the door. But it had just come back at him as his door didn't really shut properly unless you closed it carefully, jiggling the handle up as you did it. So he'd had to do that after his slam, which felt completely at odds with a show of rage.

He lay there in his onesie – a zebra one, with ears and a tail, which was too big for him because it had been passed down from Lukas – and stared at his room. His head hurt. He wasn't sure why that was, but he'd read in another part of the *Sunday Express* once that stress brought on headaches, and he knew that he was very stressed at the moment.

It wasn't that easy to sleep in his room at the best of times as the Bennetts lived on a main road called the A41, and Barry's room faced it. The Sisterly Entity had, of course, been given the quieter room at the back facing the garden, which was BIGGER as well: some rubbish about them needing to have the bigger room because there were two of them. Barry did not recognise this.

As each vehicle went past, it would light up a different section of Barry's room, depending on which way it was going.

A car driving down the road would light up his wardrobe, or DEJN NORDESBRUKK as it had been called in IKEA.

A car driving *up* the road would illuminate the ceiling and the browny-yellow patch of damp immediately above Barry's bed, which he sometimes pretended was a map of Russia that he had to study for a secret mission.

A car turning into the road from the other side would throw a sweep of white light across the far wall, which had a James Bond poster on it – Daniel Craig in a tuxedo – and another poster, of FC Barcelona, which was a couple of years out of date but still had Lionel Messi sitting in the front row. Barry had always liked the way that both of his heroes stared out of the posters with intense eyes: Lionel like he was ready to go and beat eleven players single-handedly and score with a back-heel chip, and James Bond like he was ready to kill someone.

Every so often, his bed would shake as a lorry went by.

But today he wasn't trying to get to sleep anyway. He was too angry. And he knew that, if he went to sleep, by tomorrow the argument would all be forgotten about, and he didn't want that. He had meant it. In his anger, he had come to a deep and important realisation: *his parents just weren't very good parents*. It made him sad to have this thought – his tummy fell as the words appeared in his mind, like it sometimes did when he was scared – but another part of him felt brave: like he was facing up to something.

"I wish I had better parents…" he whispered. He could feel, as he said it, a tiny tear squeeze out of his left eye. It blurred his vision, making the damp patch look less like a map of Russia and more like a smear of poo. This got in the way of his train of thought a little. It was very distracting, the idea of someone somehow getting their bottom on the ceiling to plop upside down, and so, to get back into the moment, he repeated, slightly more loudly: "I wish I had better parents."

Then, from underneath his pillow, he grabbed the list he'd secretly written down of all the things that made his mum and dad a bit rubbish at their basic job of being his mum and dad. He held it up above his face and said, a third time, the loudest so far: *"I wish I had better parents!"*

And then suddenly the entire room started to shake.

The walls were shaking like crazy; it was as if Barry's bedroom had a really bad fever. The windows rattled and his little Aston Martin DB6 model car fell off the shelf behind his bed. Barry had never been in an earthquake, but he had seen them on the telly, and thought this must be what they were like. He clutched his duvet (MYSA ROSØNGLIM, white) in fear, frightened that maybe this was happening because of what he'd just said out loud.

He was about to say, "I'm sorry, I'm sorry, I didn't mean it!" (he didn't quite know who this was addressed to – his parents, even though they weren't in the room, or, he supposed, God) when he realised... *Oh, of course: it's a lorry.*

He sat up.

It must be a very big lorry, he thought as

the room continued to shake. *It must have really powerful headlights as well*, he thought next as the far wall, the one with the posters on it, began to glow. What was odd about this glow, though, was that – unlike what usually happened when a lorry or a big car turned on to the road, which was that its headlights would light up the whole wall as the vehicle moved past – only the area around his posters seemed to be glowing.

And the glow wasn't moving. Nor was it fading. If anything, it was getting *brighter*. Maybe the lorry had stopped outside the house? Barry did notice that the shaking seemed to have died down. But you weren't allowed to stop on the A41.

As he continued to look at the posters, a very strange thing happened. Lionel Messi's and James Bond's stares seemed to turn towards him. Like they were looking at him.

And then an even stranger thing happened.

Lionel Messi said: "Barry! Hey!"

Lionel didn't move from his sitting position, in

between Iniesta and David Villa (see: told you it was out of date), with his hands on his knees. But his mouth did move. Definitely.

Barry, shocked and frightened, said nothing. But, through the shock and fear, he was also very, very curious. So he didn't look away.

"Eh! El Barrito!" said Lionel. "*Ven aquí! Rápido!*"

"He means come over here. Quickly," said another voice. A voice Barry recognised.

Barry moved his eyes sideways. James Bond was in exactly the same position he always was, but he had, quite clearly, raised his left eyebrow.

"He does?" said Barry hoarsely.

"Yes. I speak Spanish," replied James Bond. "And French, and German, and Italian, and Mandarin, and a smattering of Portuguese. Should be better, but y'know: very little action in Portugal."

"...Right," said Barry, who by now was wondering if he should just start screaming.

James Bond raised his other eyebrow. Something that Jake couldn't do. "So?"

"So... what?"

"So come over here! Like he says! Otherwise I might just have to shoot you..."

Barry gulped. He thought it best to go along with it. So he got out of bed and walked towards the glowing wall.

"I wish I had better parents!" Barry said, a third time. And then suddenly the entire room started to shake...

Barry Bennett hates being called Barry. In fact it's number 2 on the list of things he blames his parents for, along with 1) 'being boring' and 3) 'always being tired'.

But there is a world, not far from this one, where parents don't just *have* children. That's *far* too random for something so *big* and important. In this world, children are allowed to *choose* their parents.

For Barry Bennett, this world seems like a dream come true. Only things turn out to be not quite that simple...

ANiMALCOLM

◇ LIFE AS AN ANIMAL IS *WILD*... ◇

ILLUSTRATED BY
JIM FIELD

DAVID
BADDIEL

BESTSELLING AUTHOR OF **THE PARENT AGENCY**

MALCOLM DOESN'T LIKE ANIMALS.

Which is a problem because his family love them.
Their house is full of pets. What the house is NOT
full of is stuff Malcolm likes. Such as the laptop
he wanted for his birthday.

The only bright spot on the horizon is the
Year Six school trip, to . . . Oh no. A *farm*.

Over the next few days, Malcolm changes.
He learns what it's really like to be an animal.
A whole series of animals, in fact . . .

It does make him think differently. And speak
differently. And eat differently. And, um, smell
differently. But will he end up the same as before?

Because sometimes the hardest thing to
become is . . . yourself.